DANCING THROUGH LIFE
BOOK SIX

BEAUTIFUL Questions

PATRICIA M. ROBERTSON

Chapter 1

Gwen sat on her hands as Pastor Joe looked over her application. Where was the easy-going smile she was used to seeing on Sundays? Instead his eyebrows crinkled, his lips remained firm in a straight line, neither going up nor down to indicate his thoughts. Did she dare break the silence?

"So," Pastor Joe sighed as he pushed the application aside and looked at her. "Why do you want to be a church secretary?"

Gwen was prepared for this question. "I've been a member of this church for most of my life. I love the church. I thought I might do some good."

"Oh," Pastor Joe's eyes bore into her as if searching out her very soul. This was a side of the pastor Gwen was not familiar with. So intense. "You and Marcie are friends."

"Best buds." Gwen wasn't sure whether this was a selling point or not. Marcie had been the previous secretary. She had left after only six months in order to go back to college.

"I don't know what Marcie told you, but it won't be like that. No time for daydreaming or playing on your computer. The church year is picking up. Sunday school is starting again, other church activities. You won't have the free time Marcie had over the summer."

"I know, Pastor. That's what I want. I'm a good worker. I'd rather be busy than bored."

"You don't have any previous work experience."

"I know, but I have good references. I've done well in school." Gwen looked over at Pastor Joe. How much did he know? How much dare she tell? "I've been busy taking care of my mom."

"Yes, I'm aware of that." What would Pastor Joe do? He had taken on Marcie last spring as a favor to Marcie's dad. Gwen was aware how that had ended. Six months later and he's back looking for another secretary. He picked up her application again. "How will you fit in work with school and your family responsibilities?"

"I can take classes at night and my mom's doing much better or I wouldn't be here."

"And when do you graduate? What are you going to do after that?"

"I graduate in the spring, but I promise, I won't leave you without notice. I'll give you a month, two months' notice, before I leave, if I leave." Pastor Joe tapped his finger on the desk as he thought.

Gwen shifted up and down on her hands then broke the silence. "Please, Pastor, I really need this job. If I don't get out of that house, I'll go crazy. I'll work harder than anyone else could or would. I'll work overtime, no charge. I'll work late, weekends, whatever it takes to get the job done. Just give me a chance. I'll be the best secretary you've ever had."

Pastor Joe shook his head and looked at her application. Gwen could see the doubt in his eyes. She knew about Edna, his secretary before Marcie. Edna had been the best secretary he had ever had. Gwen knew that, but she was convinced that, given the opportunity, she could do better. She watched him look over her application and think.

"Okay," Pastor Joe put down the paper, "I'll think about it and let you know in a day or so."

"Thank you, Pastor." Gwen stood up and reached out her hand across the desk. Joe didn't accept the offer, sending her away with a flick of his wrist.

"Wait," Pastor Joe stopped her. "You aren't a writer, are you?

"No, Pastor. I'm an actress."

Now that the interview was over, Gwen wasn't sure she wanted the job anymore. Pastor Joe had seemed so different from all of her other interactions with him. Formal, distant, demanding. Not the warm, huggable man she met each Sunday. Was it all a sham? Which was the real pastor? Now she understood Marcie's dislike of Pastor Joe at first. Marcie, if only she could talk to her best friend, but she was away at school. It was only a four-hour drive, but it might as well be light years. Marcie was moving on with her life while she was stuck here in Cascade Falls. Everyone, all of their friends from high school, had moved on, either to school or jobs in other cities. There was nothing to keep them here, no jobs, no opportunities. And here she was stuck.

Gwen noticed the pair of tennis shoes dangling from the overhead wire. Maybe she should have taken up Marcie's offer to knock them down. Over the summer it had been fun to hear Marcie wonder about why and how they had been launched to their heights. Now they seemed to taunt her. They were a reminder of how she was stuck, stuck in this town where the best job she could get was that of a church secretary – and a part-time one at that.

Marcie had always been full of fun, creating adventures wherever she went. Only Marcie could make a mystery out of a pair of tennis shoes dangling from a wire. Only Marcie made her life bearable. That was why she needed this job. She needed it so she could make some money, put it aside and finally get out of here. Of course, she couldn't tell the pastor that. He would never hire her if he knew the truth. But she did mean what she had told him about working hard. She would show him. She would show everybody, if only she got the chance. Just give her a chance.

"Marcie, call me. I had the interview with Pastor Stick-Up-His-Butt. You were right. Call me." Gwen left the message on Marcie's phone. She was probably in class, where Gwen ought to be except she had already arranged her schedule in anticipation of getting the job. She had to get it.

Chapter 2

"So, how did the interview go?" Kathleen asked Joe at their weekly dinner. Kathleen and Joe had been dating off and on for several years. It was common knowledge in the community and yet not officially recognized as they had chosen to try to keep their relationship a secret, away from prying eyes.

"Oh, you know. She has no experience, is a college senior just looking for a job, a stopgap to fill her time and earn a little money before going on with her real life."

"That good? And she told you that?"

"She didn't have to tell me. It's obvious to anyone."

"What are you going to do? Do you have any other applicants?"

"Only ones that are even less qualified. High school drop-outs who can't string together a complete sentence. If only I could talk Edna into coming out of retirement ..." Edna had already helped to fill in the gap left by Marcie's departure. He wondered if there was a way he could keep the position open indefinitely in order to keep her on.

"You can't keep Edna by not hiring anyone else."

"Why not? I'll just tell her I haven't found anyone suitable. What's the harm in that?"

"Because Edna is smarter than that. She can see through that tactic. And she knows you've been interviewing candidates." Kathleen shook her head as she spoke. "No, better to make a good effort to fill the position than risk alienating Edna. You want to stay in her good graces for when the inevitable happens."

"What's that?"

"For when this young lady leaves."

"I guess." Joe didn't want to talk about it anymore. He knew what he had to do. He just wasn't happy about it. "What would we talk about if we didn't talk about this?"

"What are you talking about?"

"If we didn't talk about the church secretary, or my lack of one, what would we talk about?"

"We talk about other things. The dance studio. Our kids." Kathleen was the director for a local Center for the Arts, which included Joy's Dance Studio. She had inherited the title and the building when her sister-in-law, Joy, had died four years ago. Joe served on its board of directors. Kathleen's two boys, Josh and Scott, were friends with Joe's daughters, Stephanie and Michelle. All four were away at college. This was Michelle's first year. Stephanie and Scott were juniors and Josh was a fifth-year senior.

"But after that. What do we have to talk about? We talk about our kids, the Dance studio, my problems getting a secretary, but after that. What do we have to talk about?"

"We are both involved with the Human Trafficking Network."

"After that. Is that enough to build a relationship on?"

"What are you saying?" Kathleen put down her fork. Joe could tell she was wondering where this conversation was going. So was he. He wasn't sure why he was being difficult. He just was.

"I'm saying, where is this going?"

"Where is what going?" Kathleen dropped her napkin and ducked down to pick it up.

Joe waited for her to sit back up. When she remained under the table, he stooped down to join her, picking up her napkin and placing it on the table. He took her hand and pulled her back up.

"I'm asking, where is this going? This relationship? Where are we going?"

Kathleen fumbled for the napkin, knocking it off the table again. Joe reached for her hands and kept her from going back down after it.

"Look at the time." Kathleen stacked the dirty dishes. "Don't you think we should clean up?"

"Kathleen," Joe covered her hands with his. "You know what I'm talking about. Where are we going?"

"Why do we have to go anywhere? Why can't we continue as we are?"

"Because I want more. I need more. No more sneaking around. I want others to know we are a couple."

"Even if it causes you problems?" Kathleen had a questionable past. She had not been a likely candidate for Joe to fall in love with, but fall he had.

"Nothing I can't handle. I want to be able to plan a future together."

"Joe," Kathleen looked down at her hands, hidden by his. "Joe, you know I love you, but I can't do this."

"Why not?"

"I don't know. I just can't. And if you loved me, you wouldn't pressure me."

"I don't want to pressure you —"

"But you are."

"—I just, I can't go on as we are. I have to know if we are going anywhere. Do you see a future for us?"

"You know I'm not one for planning ahead. Why can't we just live in the moment?"

"Because it's not enough for me." Joe removed his hands from hers.

"Then does this mean ...?"

"I don't see us going anywhere else."

"Oh," Kathleen took her hands off the table and placed them in her lap. "We can still be friends, can't we?"

"We aren't kids, Kathleen. We are two adults, let's be adult about this. We can still be friends."

"Do you want me to help you with the dishes?"

"No, that's all right. I'll take care of it."

"At least let me clear away the dirty dishes." Kathleen stood up and finished stacking the plates. She fumbled for the silverware, placed them on the plates, picked the plates up and dropped them, sending the silverware across the floor.

"I'm so sorry." Kathleen bent down to pick up the scattered silverware. "The plates didn't break," she said as she placed the silverware back on them. Joe knelt down on the floor to help her. He put his hand on hers.

"I'll take care of this," he assured her.

"Then I guess I better go." Kathleen stood up. "I'll let myself out." Joe watched as Kathleen rushed for the door, neglecting to pick up her coat and purse from where she had tossed them on the sofa earlier.

"Kathleen, wait ..." Joe remained crouched on the floor, picking up the plates and silverware. His words hung unheard in the air. He stood up, placed the plates back on the table then walked into the living room. He picked up her coat and purse and watched the lights of her car depart into darkness.

Chapter 3

"You tried to tell me, but I didn't listen," Gwen told Marcie when they finally connected that night after Gwen's class.

"Yes, but he's really not that bad a boss." Marcie had been a reluctant secretary after dropping out of college. She had since decided on a career in journalism and was back in school. Pastor Joe had been helpful in the process. Marcie had learned to appreciate the matter-of-fact gruffness he had portrayed as a boss. It had been what Marcie had needed at that time in her life. Gwen was aware of this but still hadn't believed her.

"No. He's different as a boss. Not at all what I expected."

"You haven't gotten the job yet."

"I don't know that I want it anymore."

"Then how are you going to make money?"

"I can work at McDonald's or the Stop and Go. They always have signs that they are hiring."

"There's a reason why they are always looking for new employees. Think about it. If they were great places to work, do you think they would have so much turnover?"

"Well, the position of church secretary doesn't seem to be much better."

"Give it a chance, if you get it."

"If I get it." Gwen was sure that was not going to happen.

Word got out fast about the non-breakup of the non-couple. Kathleen refused to talk to anyone about it.

When Joe called about her coat and purse, Kathleen did not accept the call, letting it go to voice mail. She called back at a time she knew he would be busy and left a voice message, asking him to drop them off at the dance studio and giving him a time when she knew she wouldn't be there. Joe had ignored her instructions and brought them by her home. When Kathleen saw his car pull into the driveway, she begged her mother to lie for her.

"She's not here," Esther told Joe, "but thank you for dropping these off." Esther stepped out on the porch and closed the door, checking to see if Kathleen were watching. "What happened?"

"What do you know?" Joe asked.

"Not a lot. Kathleen doesn't tell me much but I can tell something's up."

"It seems we've broken up."

"I'm sorry to hear that."

"Well, how can you break up when you were never officially going together?"

"That doesn't make it any less real, or less difficult."

"Yeah, well, you know Kathleen."

"That I do. Don't give up on her. Look how many years I had to wait for her to come around." Kathleen had been a hell-raiser while in high school, went off to Chicago after graduation and had spent some time in jail before finally coming home at the age of thirty-five. "She'll come around," Esther assured Joe.

"I don't have that much time."

Kathleen watched from the window of her sons' room. She had had the option of moving upstairs from her basement bedroom when they went away to college, but chose to remain below, preserving this room for whenever they came home. Besides, this way she was removed from the view of her mother, step-father and grandfather. It wasn't the ideal living situation but it did have its advantages she realized as she waited for Joe to depart in his car.

Why was it taking so long, she wondered? What was her mom saying? What was Joe telling her? She was grateful to have her mom to act as a barrier between her and the pastor. The other advantage of living in her mom's home was that she didn't have to eat her own cooking. It wasn't enough to completely off-set the disadvantages of living in a "geriatric word," but it helped.

Kathleen watched Joe's car drive away before venturing back down stairs.

"What was that all about?" Esther asked her.

"What did Joe tell you?"

"That you had broken up?"

"How can you break up when you were never together?"

"That's what he said."

"Oh," for some reason hearing it from Joe, even second-hand, seemed like an affront, like the past few years didn't matter. "There you have it. What never started is over. No big deal."

"Saying so doesn't make it so."

"Well it is." Kathleen refused to discuss it further.

News of the non-breakup spread quickly through the dance studio. Chloe picked up on it immediately, cornering Kathleen in her office.

"What's going on?" Chloe blocked the door to keep Kathleen from leaving.

"Nothing's going on."

"Don't lie to me. I can tell something is wrong."

"There's nothing to tell, because there was nothing going on in the first place."

"What are you talking about?"

"Me and Joe. There was nothing to start with so nothing now that it's over."

"You and Pastor Joe broke up?"

"How can you break up when you weren't ever together?" Kathleen was getting tired of trying to explain. It would have been so much easier if they had officially been going out and officially broke up. This non-existent relationship and break up was harder to deal with than the real thing.

"I'm sorry to hear that," Chloe said.

"Well, life happens. Time to get on with it. Don't you have lessons to teach? And I have parents to butter up."

"Whatever you say. I'm still sorry."

"No need to be." If she said it enough, maybe she would believe it herself, Kathleen thought.

Even the teen instructors noticed something was going on.

"The witch is even witchier," they laughed to each other. "She doesn't need a costume for Halloween."

"Yeah, all she needs is her broom."

"What are you talking about?" Kathleen interrupted the group. "Aren't you supposed to be in the classroom? I'm not paying you to gab." The girls scattered to their respective classrooms, still giggling to each other. Kathleen inflicted fear into their hearts and yet she didn't as they were able to see through her tough exterior. Still they knew better than to cross her.

Ashley was the only one who wasn't bothered by the non-breakup.

"That's okay, Aunt Kathleen. I know about you and Pastor Joe. I never really liked him," Ashley told her over burgers on their regular monthly sleep-over night. Ever since the death of Ashley's mom Joy, Kathleen had taken Ashley out to the place of her choice, then she spent the night.

"You didn't?" Kathleen was surprised. Everybody liked Joe.

"Oh, he's okay. I guess. But not for you. Besides, he came over all the time when mom was sick. She liked his visits. I didn't."

"Why not?"

"Because I knew it meant my mom was dying. He's like the grim reaper."

"I thought you saw him for a while, for counseling?"

"I did. He's okay for that. He's just not the right guy for you."

"And who would be right for me?"

"I don't know. I haven't met him yet. But when I do, I'll let you know."

"Hmmm, my own matchmaker."

"No, more like relationship coach," Ashley stated. Kathleen spit out her Coke as she laughed.

"So, I'm to get relationship advice from a twelve-year-old."

"A precocious twelve-year-old. You said so yourself."

"Yes, I did. Finish your burger."

Chapter 4

Gwen was reveling in her theater classes. She had completed the requirements for her associates degree at the local community college. While there she had pursued a general course of study, fulfilling her pre-requisites as she struggled to decide on a major. She had started in social work at the community college but switched it to her minor when she transferred. Social work had seemed as good a major as any at the time. It seemed like she was already a social worker as she took care of her mother. She certainly knew about being a caretaker for others. She had liked the classes at first – until they started to feel like another trap.

She was already trapped at home taking care of her mom. Did she really want to spend the rest of her life taking care of others? She didn't think so. She had tentatively taken one theater class at the community college just for fun, as an elective, and had been bitten. The theater bug sank its teeth deep into her arm where she had not been able to dislodge it despite her best efforts. Best to give in, she decided. She met with the chair of the theater department before transferring and had been sufficiently impressed to sign up.

She had a full range of theater classes to fill her schedule and a few social work classes to complete her minor. The classes required most of her evenings as she participated in productions, bit parts as she learned about make-up, costumes and set designs. She particularly liked working with costumes, volunteering to organize and maintain the costumes for the small theater department. She quickly got to know the other students and teachers in the department as they became a second family to her, a tight knit community.

They helped to make up for missing Marcie and were a surrogate family in place of the dysfunctional one that was hers. Her social work classes had helped put terms to what she already knew and experienced. Dysfunctional families – they were more the norm than the exception.

Acting was a good partner to social work, or so she thought. If she had been a social worker all her life, taking care of her mom, she had also been an actress, putting on a happy face to hide what was going on at home. Putting on a false face to the rest of the community lest anyone know the reality of her existence – that the good doctor's family wasn't the epitome of perfection. She almost convinced herself of this, that what she was experiencing was normal. She created the illusion of normalcy for the rest of the world to see. That had been her job – that and massaging her mom's bruised ego and tending to her during her fits of depression. It had not been much of a life.

How much did Pastor Joe know about this? She didn't know. Except for the brief mention during her interview, he had never given any indication of knowing more. She figured it was best that way.

She had been surprised when Pastor Joe called and offered her the position two days after the interview, and even more surprised when she heard herself accept the job.

If it didn't work out, she could always quit, she told herself.

"You won't regret it," Gwen assured the pastor.

Chapter 5

"I hope not," Joe said after hanging up. He was already regretting the conversation with Kathleen. He didn't need another regret.

Pastor Joe was pleasantly surprised when Gwen proved to be as good as her word. Where Marcie had played on her phone and computer, Gwen didn't waste a minute, looking for more work once she had her work done. Where Marcie skipped out early and came up with excuses to be gone for hours at a time, Gwen stayed late if needed.

At least something in his life was going well. Joe wasn't sure why he had forced the point with Kathleen, but he had and there was no going back. Maybe it was just as well. He had always known this relationship was doomed from the start. Two unlikely partners. He ought to know, with all of the marriage prep and marriage counseling he did. It was hard enough to make a relationship work when there was a high level of compatibility. He and Kathleen had little in common. In fact, as he thought about it, it seemed the main factor that brought them together was that they were both single and the proximate age. That was a big plus in this city where so many singles paired up in high school or college. Where did the out-of-college male or female find a mate besides the workplace, church or a bar? Granted, the dating pool was ever changing now that divorce was so common and many were waiting until they were older to settle down. Still it remained a challenge to find a suitable date once you reached a certain age.

"Don't worry. The older you get, the bigger the pool to fish from." One of his elderly parishioners had assured him. Older women outnumbered men by four to one.

"If you can't find anybody with those odds, then there's no chance for you, pastor," the man teased.

"So how long do I have to wait?" Joe asked.

"Well, let's see. You're in your forties ... give it twenty or thirty years or so. By then there'll be plenty of widows and divorcees. You'll have your pick." The man had laughed and poked him in the ribs. Joe was only able to manage a weak smile in return.

"Sure, Pastor," another of the group of older men added. "You've got the best years of your life ahead of you, if only you can live that long."

Joe did not want to wait that long to start living again. When he had first come to Cascade Falls, there had been a parade of meat loaves and lasagnas brought by eager single women, some newly divorced, others who had passed that golden age of thirty without a ring and were beginning to think it would never happen. He had fended them off by pretending to date Ava, who had newly arrived from Nebraska to teach seventh grade. It had been a relationship of convenience for both. Neither had been ready to date anyone seriously. Both had skeletons from prior relationships that had been keeping them from seeking out another one, him from the sudden death of his wife, Ava from her divorce.

Then Ava started dating Dale Reese and he quietly started seeing Dale's sister Kathleen in an on-again/off-again relationship. They tried to keep the relationship private, between the two of them, going separately to city events, meeting at restaurants in various towns, slipping over to each other's homes. Joe had Kathleen park a block away and sneak in through the side door in the hope that no one would be the wiser. When he came to Kathleen's home, they pretended it was just a pastoral visit since Kathleen lived with her mother, a church member. If anyone complained that the Reese family was getting more than their share of the pastor's attention, they kept it to themselves, or among the gossip network, not daring to broach the subject with pastor.

He knew the effort was futile, that everyone knew about his relationship with Kathleen. That was part of why he wanted to finally stop the charade. Instead the relationship had ended before it had even officially begun.

Sure, there were other good fish in the sea, he told himself, but when he looked around, there was no one quite like Kathleen. He had to make his peace with that. In the meantime, at least he had a secretary he could count on. That was one less worry to deal with. He didn't have to look for a secretary and a girlfriend at the same time. Besides, he could do without a girlfriend, but not without a secretary.

Chapter 6

"Pastor Joe and the buxom brunette broke up?" Marcie asked during their regular evening phone calls. Marcie had referred to Kathleen as the buxom brunette in the blog she had written over the summer.

"I think so. She hasn't called all week. Pastor Joe seems even more wrapped up in his work, if that's possible."

"Just ask him," Marcie told her.

"I can't do that."

"Why not?"

"I just can't." Gwen wasn't sure why. She just figured it would be out-of-line for the lowly secretary to pry into her boss's private affairs. "Because I can't. That's all. Would you have asked him?"

"Sure. Just say, I notice Ms. Reese hasn't been around lately."

"I can't do that."

"Sure, you can. If you can help break up a human trafficking ring, then you can ask Pastor Joe." Gwen remembered. It had been one of the highlights of a summer filled with high points.

"That was because of you. I never would have done it without you."

"Of course, you could have done it then – and you can ask Pastor Joe about this now. This may be a good chance. You always had a thing for the good pastor."

"That was before he became my boss, before I saw his 'human' side. Though he's not as bad as I thought he was going to be." After the initial interview and the first week on the job, Pastor Joe had softened in his manner towards her. Gwen thought maybe it had something to do with the fact that she actually did her job, unlike Marcie. Having Marcie as a reference had been a mistake, she had realized too late. "You weren't exactly the best reference."

"Come on. I wasn't that bad," Marcie insisted.

"You keep telling yourself that." They talked a while longer till they had exhausted their usual topics. "I can't wait till you come home. You are coming home for Thanksgiving, aren't you? You aren't running off to visit Bernie?" Bernie, Marcie's on-again/off-again boyfriend, and Marcie had split up at the end of the summer when he went back to Nashville to play in a country band.

"It wouldn't be Thanksgiving without seeing you," they both agreed.

"Why can't we go to the Reeses' for Thanksgiving this year? We didn't break up with anyone. We are still friends with Josh and Scott." Joe's daughters were whining at the prospect of Thanksgiving with him.

"I'll fix a turkey and we'll do Stove-Top stuffing. You always loved my stuffing. It will be like it used to be."

"And it will be just as lame now as it was back then," Stephanie said.

"I thought you liked our Thanksgivings together."

"That was because we didn't know we had other options," Stephanie said.

"Yeah, really, Dad," Michelle added.

"Okay. I realize Thanksgiving with Josh and Scott is a lot more fun than Thanksgiving with your dad but humor me. Besides, we're not invited."

"Sure, we are. Scott invited us. Can't Michelle and I go by ourselves?"

"And leave me alone on Thanksgiving?"

"Maybe you should have thought about that before breaking up with Scott's mom," Stephanie said.

"Hey, she broke up with me."

"Whatever. I just don't see why we should be punished for your poor relationship skills," Stephanie said.

"You'd really leave me alone on Thanksgiving?"

"We'd rather you came along with us, but if not, that's your problem."

"OMG, Dad. You said yourself that you and Kathleen were still friends —" Michelle decided to join the conversation.

"— Well, I lied."

"— Why can't you get along for a few hours? There will be lots of other people there. You won't even have to say a word to her if you don't want to."

"Are you sure that I'm even welcome?"

"Of course, you are. I'll check with Scott," Stephanie assured him.

"Okay, if it means that much to you." Joe agreed.

"We're coming," Stephanie called Scott. "Now you have to clear it with your mom."

"No problem," Scott assured her. "Good news," he announced to the others at the table. "Stephanie, Michelle and their dad can come after all."

"Oh," Kathleen stopped eating and looked up. "Who invited them?"

"I did," Scott said.

"And I told him to. It just wouldn't be the same without them. You two can get along for one day," Esther told her.

"I guess." Kathleen picked at her food, keeping her gaze fixed back on her plate.

"Good. Then it's settled." Esther stood up. "I have some pies to start making."

Chapter 7

Laura awoke. What day was it? Did it matter? She wanted to remain in the cocoon that was her bed, wrapped in warmth and oblivion. It took too much effort to get up, get dressed only to crawl back into bed twelve hours later. Why not just stay there? Made more sense, not that she ever made much sense before.

What day was it? Did it make a difference? She felt the empty space that had held her husband's sleeping body. Gone. Like every other day. Walter was up early and gone before she got out of bed, if she got out of bed. Why should today be any different from any other day? She had this niggling suspicion that something was going to happen today, but she couldn't pin it down. Soon her daughter would come into the room, pull away her covers and make her get up. Doctor's orders, she told herself. You have to get up every day. You have to exercise, move around, get out in nature, out in the sun. Yeah, yeah, yeah. Easy for him to say.

"Exercise, fresh air, sunlight, a healthy diet. They are all essential components of a full recovery."

"Yeah, sure. Whatever you say," she had said inside. On the outside she heard a voice say, "Yes, doctor." Whose voice was that? She guessed it was hers but she wondered. She would say anything, agree to anything, to keep from being put back into the hospital.

The hospital wasn't so bad, another voice told her. No responsibilities. You didn't have to look at your daughter and husband and be reminded what a failure you were. No, better to roll back over in bed and hide from reality in sleep.

"Mom, get up," her daughter's voice called from somewhere in the distance. She was far away, Laura told herself, until she felt the covers pulled away. Bereft of her cavernous escape, the voice no longer echoed in the distance but was present, in her face.

"Mom, get up. It's Thanksgiving."

Oh, that's it. She knew there was something different about today. "Is my Elizabeth coming? And the boys, Douglas and Clayton?"

"No, Mom. Remember. They aren't coming. They live too far away." Gwen hated making excuses for her siblings, and Laura knew that. She could tell Gwen was lying. Gwen would say whatever it took to get her out of bed.

"Then I don't need to get up." Laura pulled the covers back.

"Yes, you do. Remember Marcie and her dad are coming over. It was your idea."

"It was?" Laura slowly sat up, as she allowed the words to sink in.

"Yes, it was. None more surprised than me. Now get up."

There had been a time when her mom had enjoyed entertaining company. Gwen didn't remember exactly when that had changed. Maybe about the time her sister Betsy had left for college and never looked back. But even before that there had been signs of the retreat into darkness. Betsy was six years older than Gwen. She had idolized her big sister but her big sister had little to do with her, especially once on her own. Betsy had found convenient excuses to stay at college after her freshman year. She had a job that kept her away from home. Gwen's older brothers had been better about coming home from college at first. They were eight and ten years older than her. They had been the object of their mom's affections, which she lavished on them, leaving nothing for her, or so it seemed to Gwen.

It had been fun at first, when they would come home from college. That was back when they still celebrated Thanksgiving. Mom had been at her best on those occasions, pouring out love upon the turkey till it basted to a golden brown. Getting up early to stuff the bird and put it in the oven while her boys, newly arrived from college, slept in. They were woken to a big breakfast of sausage, eggs and muffins. She and Elizabeth had been her mom's servant those days, helping her in the kitchen while the men watched football.

Her sister, Betsy, had always been "my Elizabeth," as her mother had a proprietary claim on each of her children, making them in her own image and likeness. As long as Elizabeth was still home, Gwen escaped the intense focus that was her mom. It seemed her mom only had two ways of being a mom. She either focused all of her attention on you to the point of suffocation, or there was benign neglect. There was no in-between for Mom that Gwen could detect. If given the choice, she preferred the benign neglect. She was able to come and go as she pleased, while her sister bore the brunt of her mom's obsessions.

This ended when her sister left for college. Then her mom had no one left to focus on but her. But once her three oldest children were gone, it seemed something else departed with them, the light in her mom's eyes. The brief episodes of depression that had been kept at bay by the presence of a full house of children, collapsed into months of staring off into space, barely making an effort. Just getting out of bed proved too much for her mom on many days. Gwen would get herself off to school, come home and find her mom still in bed or sitting in the living room with shades pulled and the TV on.

Gwen's dad was a minor player in the drama that unfolded in the house he paid for. His job as a doctor was demanding and gave him the perfect excuse to avoid the progression of decay in his relationship with her mother, or so Gwen thought. Or maybe it was Gwen's excuse, allowing her to pretend everything was okay, that it was normal for her dad to be gone all the time.

Gwen remembered how it had been at first, when they had first moved here. Then her mom had been fine. She dressed up for every occasion, even non-occasions. She would take an ordinary day and work her magic with Hawaiian Luas in the dead of winter, princess tea parties and teddy bear tea parties in the summer. She had been the fun mom, but even then, Gwen had known something was not right. Her best friend, Marcie, had loved her mom, but she didn't see all that

Gwen saw. She wasn't there at bed time when her mom and dad fought, or when her mom fought with her sister. For some reason, her mom never fought with her brothers. It seemed they were golden in her eyes. They could do no wrong as she fussed over and petted them. Elizabeth could do no right, nor could her dad. Gwen was happy to slip off to bed by herself to escape the noise.

There were times, though, back then, when her mom and dad would dress up and go out to restaurants for dinner parties. And there was the annual hospital fundraiser, a formal occasion. Her mom had looked like a princess as she rode off with her prince, Gwen's dad. Her dad would tell her mom how beautiful she looked and help her with her wrap. Her mom would laugh, accepting his worship as her right. They would waltz out into the night as stars glistened above. Gwen had watched the fairy tale adventure. They would come home late and sometimes her mom would wake her up to tell her about the night and give her the piece of cake she had brought home for her.

"It was wonderful. I just can't sleep," her mom would say as Gwen sat up in bed and listened to her mom talk about the gala event – who was there, what they wore. Gwen hung on every word, feeling special to be included in the magic. She dreamed of someday going to a ball herself.

"Do you think I could go with you, Mama? When I'm older?"

"Of course, you can, when you are older. You are my Princess Gwendolyn after all." Those had been good times. She had been a princess, her sister Elizabeth was the queen, the boys the crown princes, but her mom ruled over all.

Other times though Gwen was woken by her parents' fighting.

"You were flirting with her," she heard her mother's voice floating up the stairs.

"Don't be ridiculous," her dad countered. "She's a benefactor. I have to smoosh her so she'll give more to the oncology wing we are building."

"It was more than smooshing. And all those pretty little nurses. Are they benefactors too?" Her mother's voice continued to rise up the stairs.

"Shhh, Laura, you'll wake the kids. You don't want the whole neighborhood to hear you." Gwen heard her dad try to calm her mom. "Those nurses are my staff. Maybe next year it will be better if you didn't come."

"Maybe I won't," Gwen heard her mom say. Gwen knew it wouldn't happen. Her mom loved this affair, loved getting dressed up, having her hair done, her nails polished. Her mom loved everything about the night. There was no way she would miss it, would she?

Gwen got up the next morning and tiptoed downstairs to the kitchen. She didn't want her brothers or sister to wake up. There it was, her piece of cake wrapped in foil and sitting on the table. Gwen slowly pulled back the foil, trying to be as quiet as possible lest her brothers get up and eat the cake in one big gulp as they were known to do.

It was beautiful as she knew it would be — yellow cake with white frosting and pink flowers. Gwen put a finger to the frosting. Did she dare?

"Go ahead, honey." Gwen was startled by her mother's voice. She pulled her finger away. "Go ahead. I brought it home for you. You're the only one who cares. Your brothers and sister, they aren't interested in balls. But you still are my little princess. Someday they will be gone. Then it will just be you and me."

"And Daddy."

"Yes, and Daddy." Her mom sighed and pulled a fork out of the silverware drawer. "Here you go." It tasted every bit as good as it looked.

"Why were you and Daddy fighting?" Gwen asked.

"Oh, it was nothing. Mommies and Daddies fight sometimes. Nothing for you to worry about."

"What's flirting?"

"Where did you hear that?"

"I heard you last night."

"Oh, it's being very nice to someone."

"What's wrong with that?"

"You'll understand when you're older. Let me tell you about the ball."

Gwen knew her mother would never miss the ball. It was the highlight of each year, until she heard her mom fighting with her dad about going.

"Come on, Laura, get ready. I don't ask that much of you. The least you can do is put in an appearance. You know I have to attend. Don't make me go alone."

"And watch you flirt with those women?"

"You know that's my job. It's going to all these functions and networking with all these people that got me my current job." Gwen wasn't sure what networking was but she knew her dad had a new job. She hadn't bothered to ask what. It was another excuse for Dad to stay away from home.

"Laura, don't make me go alone."

Gwen tried not to hear, though sometimes she considered the loud fights better than the icy silence. She could imagine her dad taking her mom's hands into his, staring into her eyes until she said yes. That had been her freshman year in high school. By her sophomore year, her mom had become someone she didn't recognize, someone who found the effort to get dressed up too much for her.

"Fine. I'll go by myself. It would serve you right if I started fooling around with one of those women you accuse me of flirting with. Might as well have the fun since I already have the blame. I don't even recognize you anymore. What happened to the woman I married?"

Gwen was surprised when even this didn't elicit a response from her mom. The next year, Gwen got her wish. She went to the ball with her dad in place of her mom. It had not been everything that she had expected. This time it was she who brought home a piece of cake for her mom, but her mom didn't eat it.

"Just leave it for me, honey. I'll eat it in the morning," she had told Gwen. In the morning, Gwen found the cake thrown in the garbage.

There was no way Gwen was going to let her mom sleep through another Thanksgiving. She had been surprised when her mom had suggested inviting Marcie and her dad over.

"Even with a small turkey, we'll have way more than we can eat," her mom had said.

"Mom, I've got the turkey in the oven. I'll take care of everything. All you have to do is get dressed and come downstairs."

"Where's your father?"

"He had to go into work for a while this morning. He'll be home by noon. Now get up. Do you want me to get the shower ready?"

"No, sweetie." Laura pushed back the covers and slid her legs over the side of the bed. "I can do it myself."

Even with this assurance, Gwen was worried whether her mother would make it downstairs for dinner.

Her dad came home by noon and offered to help in the kitchen. Gwen put him to work fixing the sweet potatoes while she prepared green bean casserole. The scent of turkey permeated the house, seeking out the farthest corners of the downstairs living area and creeping up into the upstairs bedrooms till everything smelled of Thanksgiving. Marcie and her dad were supposed to come around two o'clock. They were bringing dessert. Gwen was keeping it simple: turkey, stuffing, sweet potatoes, and green beans.

"Where's your mother?"

"She better be taking a shower. Do you want me to check on her?"

"No, that's all right. I'll do it." Her dad came back and confirmed that her mom was getting ready.

"Guess that's all we can ask for," Gwen said.

"Oh, we could ask for a whole lot more, but for now, we'll take what we get."

Marcie and her dad arrived promptly at two. Gwen hurried from the kitchen when the doorbell rang.

"Something smells great, Gwen," said Henry, Marcie's dad, as he walked through the door.

"That would be turkey. Hard to ruin turkey. You just put it in the oven till the timer pops up."

"Well, we've had some adventures with turkey, haven't we, Marcie?"

"Yes, if you hadn't invited us, we'd probably be eating at the local Denny's, or frying burgers. We gave up on cooking Thanksgiving dinner years ago." Marcie held up a pumpkin pie. "Where do you want me to put this?" she asked.

"Homemade?" Gwen asked.

"By the local bakery," Henry said. "And we brought the whip cream." Henry held up a bag with a spray can of whipped cream. "Fresh from the can. Where's your lovely wife?" Henry asked Gwen's dad.

On cue, Gwen's mother appeared at the top of the stairs. Her make-up was applied, her hair done, and she wore her favorite string of pearls with a simple black dress. She started down the stairs in her high heels. It had been months since Gwen had seen her mom dressed up.

"You look lovely, Laura," Henry said as he gave her a kiss on the cheek.

"Thank you, Henry."

"Yeah, you do," Gwen's dad said, not even attempting to cover his surprise. Her mom ignored him.

"I'm so glad you and Marcie could make it," she said. "You brought dessert? How nice. Gwen, why don't you take that pumpkin pie into the kitchen while I show our guests into the living room."

"That's okay, Mrs. Thompson. I'll help Gwen in the kitchen." Marcie followed Gwen into the kitchen while the older adults went into the living room.

"OMG! What was that?" Marcie asked as soon as the kitchen door closed.

"I know, right?" Gwen said. "I guess my mom just needed an audience. She always did like to make a grand entrance."

"And that she did."

"I just hope she can keep it up for the rest of the afternoon." Gwen pulled the turkey out to rest, then she and Marcie set the table.

Dinner went surprisingly well. Gwen's mother was her old self, telling stories and enlivening the conversation.

"You girls did a great job with dinner," Laura said as they enjoyed pumpkin pie and coffee in the living room. "Why don't you let me take care of the dishes?"

"On, no, Mom. That's okay. Dad and I can do the dishes. You need your rest."

"Nonsense. Having guests over, I'm feeling like my old self." Laura stood up and started to clear the dessert plates, the plates clinking in her shaking hands.

"Laura," Gwen's dad stood up and took the plates away from her.

"Very well. I guess I am a little tired. It was so good to see you again, Henry, Marcie. You are always welcome." Laura made her exit.

"Gwen and I will clean up," Marcie stood up. "Go home, Dad. We're going out with friends afterwards. I'll ride with Gwen."

"I guess I've been dismissed." Henry stood up to leave.

"You can stay and watch the game here," Walter suggested.

"No, that's fine. Time I headed home anyway. Thank you for dinner. Thank Laura again for me."

Walter helped the girls cleanup in the kitchen. After they left he checked on his wife. She was back under the covers.

"Laura, it was good to see you your old self. Why don't you come back downstairs? The girls are gone. It will just be you and me."

"No, Walter. I'm tired out from the charade I put on this afternoon."

"But was it all a charade? Don't you think you are getting better, bit by bit."

"Maybe. It almost felt real."

"It was real."

"Do you think we could get the kids to come home for Christmas, just this once? Have the whole family together again?"

"We can certainly try," Walter assured her.

Chapter 8

Kathleen was restless after everyone had left, leaving her with her mom, stepdad and grandfather. Another Thanksgiving night with them. At least the last two years Joe had been around. Josh and Scott were out with their friends. It was too much to ask that they hang out with family after all day with them. The day had been, okay, awkward, but okay, with her trying to avoid Joe and her mom throwing the two of them together, having Joe help in the kitchen.

"I brought us a helper." Esther led Joe into the kitchen. "Pastor Joe's going to help you peel the potatoes." Esther put a ten-pound bag of potatoes in the sink and backed away. "Okay, you two, get moving."

"Do we really need this many potatoes?" Kathleen asked.

Esther just looked at her till Kathleen grabbed a knife and started peeling.

"Here, Pastor," Esther handed him another knife. "These potatoes won't peel themselves."

Joe and Kathleen had peeled in silence while Esther checked the turkey. When she left the room Joe asked, "How have you been?"

"Okay, and you?"

"The same."

"That's good. I hear you've got a new secretary."

"Yes, I hired Gwen. She's very good." Joe reached over for another potato. "How's everything at the dance studio?"

"Oh, you know."

"The same?"

"Yes. Getting ready for the Christmas recital. How's the church?"

"Getting ready for Advent."

They fell back into silence as Esther came back into the kitchen, cut the potatoes into smaller pieces and put them into a large pot of water and set it to boil. Kathleen managed to escape at dinner by sitting with Josh, Scott, Stephanie and Michelle, while Joe sat at the head of the table with her mom and her step-dad, Peter. Other family members filled out the table, including Kathleen's brother Dale and his family, and Joy's sister Sara and her family.

After the leftovers were put away, dishes put in the dishwasher and pots and pans washed, the young adults took the kids outside to play until it was time for pie. Kathleen stepped outside on the back porch for some fresh air, watching the antics of her sons.

"I never should have come today." Kathleen had been surprised by the familiar voice.

"No, it's okay. We said we would be friends. It's time we start. We can't go on avoiding each other."

"No, I guess not."

"And besides, our kids are friends." Kathleen looked over to where Josh and Scott were showing Jacob and Grace how to throw a football. Stephanie and Michelle were watching Sara's toddlers. Sara had been Joy's baby sister. Sara, her husband, Larry, and their twins, were still an important part of the family.

"Do you think it will get easier over time?"

"I hope so," Joe said as he leaned on the railing of the porch. "I hope so."

It had been a relief when he had finally left, despite their conversation after dinner. Now, she just had to get out.

"Mom, I'm going out for a while."

"Where?"

"Just to that new brew pub that opened a month ago. The one in the neighborhood. I just want to check it out. I won't be gone long."

"Okay."

"You want to come?" Grandpop was already upstairs for the night and Peter was dozing in his chair. Kathleen felt guilty about leaving her mom alone.

"No, that's okay, honey. I'm pretty tired. Don't be late."

Why did she have to add that, Kathleen thought as she left. She was over forty, yet her mother still treated her like an errant teenager.

The brew pub was only a short drive from their house. It was one of the many such places popping up throughout the state. They already had four other similar establishments in Cascade Falls. It was in the neighborhood, like a neighborhood bar. The place was full of college-aged students escaping their parents' homes after Thanksgiving. She wondered if she would run into Josh and Scott. A quick scan of the pub let her know they were not around. Relieved she sat on a stool at the counter and looked at the variety of beer listed on the board.

"Scotch," she told the man behind the counter.

"No scotch. Just home-brewed beer. What'll you have?"

"Oh, okay. What do you recommend?" Kathleen finally settled on a stout.

"Yeah, if you want scotch you have to go to the Green Door or another bar." A man sat down next to her.

"Do I know you?" Kathleen looked him over. He appeared to be about forty, close to her age, closer than any of the youngsters in the pub.

"No, but I believe I know you. Aren't you the buxom brunette?"

"Yes, I am. How do you know me?" Kathleen continued to look him over. Who was he?

"Actually, my daughter knows you. Marcie Taylor. She had pointed you out to me before."

"You're Marcie's dad?" Kathleen didn't even try to hide the surprise that was evident on her face. She wondered what Marcie might have said about her.

"None other."

"And why would that give you the right to say you know me?"

"It doesn't. However, you're the only other person close to my age in this establishment and I hate to drink alone."

"I guess that's a good enough reason. What brings you here on Thanksgiving night?"

"I might ask you the same thing. Don't you have boys in college? Aren't they home?"

"No, they're out with friends."

"And now you know where Marcie is. Mind if I buy you a drink?" Henry placed an order. "I hadn't wanted to go home after Thanksgiving dinner. Figured it was still early. Went home for a while, but after an hour or so of rattling around in an empty house, I decided to go out for a beer," he explained. "Figured, maybe I'd try that new brewpub. So here I am, and here you are. It's fate."

"Fate," Kathleen said as she smiled and downed her beer. "Maybe it is."

Chapter 9

Christmas was on its way and Gwen was happy. She was helping with costumes for the Christmas dance recital at Joy's Dance Studio, helping with the nativity at church, and had a small part in her college's production of "A Christmas Carol." She was the specter of death. The director thought her tall, lanky frame was perfect for the part. Gwen was enjoying the creepiness of the part and practiced her slow, ghostly movements while moving about the church office. She entertained her mom with her spectral, slow dance at home. It didn't bring about a smile, but at least it had some effect. Ever since Thanksgiving her mom had showed progress. She got herself up every morning, even if only to move to the couch in the living room. At least it was progress. Her mom was looking forward to Christmas and seeing Elizabeth and Douglas. Clayton already had other plans that couldn't be changed. Her dad had contacted them on Thanksgiving and asked them to come home for Christmas.

"It will mean a lot to your mother," he had told them.

"I'll see, Dad. I'll try," and "I don't know. I'm really busy right now," were all the response he received – but it was enough. Enough so that her mom had something to look forward to, something to give her a reason to get up every morning. Gwen didn't care what that reason was. She was just glad that her mom was doing better. She may be playing the specter of death, but inside she was light and happiness.

And even more, now that her mom was doing better, she had been able to convince her dad to let her attend the winter session abroad in Guatemala. Each January her college had a short winter semester. Only three weeks, it was geared toward an intensive course of study. Students took one class that met every day, all day for three weeks. It was the perfect opportunity for a short-term "integration of faith and learning" experience, or so the course description said. Some students participated in an intensive study of urban blight, spending the time in

Chicago or New York, where they helped out at homeless shelters and saw firsthand the problems of inner cities. Others stayed on campus and others went on trips to other countries. Gwen had not been able to get away for three weeks before because of her responsibilities at home, but this year was different. Finally, a chance to travel to another country, even if it was a developing country and not Paris, or Geneva, two of her top destinations, if, when, she ever got out of Cascade Falls.

Throughout high school Gwen had missed out on any activity that required being gone for more than a day. That meant she had not gone on the trip to France sponsored by the French club, or the trip to Italy for her art classes. She had been stuck at home with her mom because her mom couldn't be left alone for that long. Gwen had run cross-country in the fall and played softball in the spring. Even those activities had been a challenge because they required her staying after school for practice and late nights at away games. Afterwards she had to rush home to make sure her mom was okay. Her dad had to rearrange his schedule to allow her to attend these events, but that meant he couldn't attend, unless her mom was well enough to be left alone.

Gwen remembered looking up into the stands as she pitched, wishing her parents were there to watch. But then the one time Dad brought Mom, it was worse than them not coming at all. Mom had showed up in Detroit Tiger regalia, cheered too loudly for too long, and brought snacks like she had done for her t-ball games.

"Whose mom is that?" her team mates had questioned after the first inning. Gwen hadn't answered, pretending she didn't know her, then felt guilty for it. When the snacks came out, there was no avoiding the obvious.

"Mom, we don't do snacks anymore," Gwen had pulled her mom aside and whispered.

"Thanks, Mrs. Thompson," her team mates said as they took juice pouches and fruit roll-ups. "These rock."

"See, dear, your friends appreciate my snacks," her mom insisted.

"Don't sweat it, Gwen. My mom was a total psycho at the spring dance," another team mate said as they walked back to the locker room.

"I can't believe how you acted," Gwen's mom confronted her when Gwen came home. "I made the effort to come to your game and you act like you didn't even know me." Gwen had been surprised that her mom had had enough energy to confront her.

"Leave the girl be." her dad had come to her rescue. "I know Gwen appreciated you being there, didn't you, Gwen?"

"Sure, thanks, Mom," Gwen said. Marcie didn't understand when Gwen complained to her.

"At least you have a mom," she had stated.

Gwen had decided to forego all sports after high school, even though she was recruited for the softball team at the community college she was attending. It was too much hassle. She did run now and then. It helped relieve her pent-up frustration.

Ever since her hospital stay over the summer, her mom had seemed to be making progress. Maybe they finally had her meds right, Gwen thought. Managing her mom's depression required a fine balance of the right medication. They would try one for a while. When that didn't work, her doctor would prescribe another. When they found one that worked, over time, it stopped working or required increasing doses. Sometimes Gwen just wanted to yell at her mom.

"Get over it. Get over yourself. Stop moping around. Do something!" Gwen knew it would do her mom no good, but it might feel good for the moment.

"A moment on the lips, a lifetime of guilt," she told herself so she had refrained.

Being a theater major had been a challenge. It required late-night rehearsals and then the shows. Gwen had managed to work it out with her dad. He would be home nights she had rehearsals and classes. And now, finally, being gone for three whole weeks! Gwen looked up at the dangling tennis shoes as she drove home from rehearsals and smiled. Finally, she was getting out of here! It was more than she could hope for. Gwen sent for her passport and spent what little free time she had reading about Guatemala.

Between work, school and other activities, Gwen was rarely home this semester, which was precisely how she liked it. She wasn't missing any opportunity to volunteer. So, when she saw they needed someone to help with the kids' Christmas program at the school and the Sunday School, she was among the first to volunteer. That was how she got to know Ava. Ava had come to Cascade Falls to teach seventh grade at St. Luke's. She had since then married Dale, Kathleen's brother, and had become a regular at the Dance Studio that had been started by Dale's former wife. Because Ava had a background in drama, the responsibility for any school program at St. Luke's fell to her.

"There's really not a whole lot to it, after all," she told Gwen. "It's the nativity. The story doesn't change, just the players," Ava told her when she first showed up. "When I first came here, I tried to spice things up a bit, change the program. That didn't go well. Now I figure – why work so hard and have no one happy afterwards? I stick to the basics and everybody is happy. The parents are happy to see their kids on stage, the kids are happy because there are punch and cookies after the play, the other teachers are happy because they don't have to be bothered with this. The principal's happy because the parents are happy, and I'm happy because I don't have to work as hard and I'm able to get home sooner," Ava explained.

"Same thing with the Sunday School program, but even more so," she added. The kids in Sunday school were the ones who couldn't afford to go to St. Luke's or who chose not to attend for whatever reason. They had to get their religious instruction some time. That time was for an hour and a half each Sunday, before the eleven a.m. service. There was also an adult Sunday school program for the parents of the children in Sunday school and anyone else who was interested. Some parents dropped their kids off to Sunday school then went back home until time for the service, others went out for breakfast, others gathered over coffee in the church hall, while others chose to take advantage of the opportunity to learn more about their faith.

"It's a life-long process," Pastor Joe told the congregation when they had sign-up Sunday. "It isn't enough to go to Sunday school as a kid or send your children. As adults we need to keep learning about our faith, keep growing in our understanding of who God is in our lives. We need to exercise our spiritual muscles." He had convinced Gwen.

Gwen didn't sign up for the Sunday school classes at church. What would be the fun in that? Sitting around with a lot of middle-aged and older adults? Instead she found herself attracted to the various Bible Studies on campus. But when to fit them in to her busy schedule?

Last year when she had taken classes in the day, she had never considered going to the chapel services or attending the fellowship groups or Bible study. Now that her classes were at night, she was feeling drawn to these groups. She didn't know why. There was an eight o'clock morning Bible study on Wednesday. She could attend and still get to work by nine or so. It was fun to be with others her age. They drank coffee, munched on donuts, and talked about God. Gwen wasn't sure about the God stuff, but she liked the coffee and donuts. When members of the study went to the nine o'clock chapel service, she asked Pastor Joe if it was okay if she came to work late on Wednesday mornings.

"I'll stay till four to make up for the time missed," she had assured him. She was already giving Pastor Joe more hours than she was being paid for but still felt the need to prove herself.

"Sure. As long as you get your work done." It was as if Pastor Joe felt an obligation to add that. Maybe he was still feeling the effect of the six months with Marcie and not ready to let down his guard with her. What would it take for him to trust her, she wondered?

When Gwen asked Pastor Joe for the three weeks off so she could go on a cross-cultural experience, she could tell he felt justified in his caution where she was concerned.

"I'll work extra hard to get everything ready before I leave, and extra hard to catch up when I get back. Please, Pastor. January's a slow time." No time was slow time in a church, she knew, but she had been such a hard worker, so reliable these past few months, how could he say no to her? She felt she had earned the time off.

"I'll see what I can work out." Pastor Joe had called Edna, his former secretary, to talk her into coming back for those three weeks, while Gwen waited. "Perhaps she can postpone her winter trip to Florida till February." He punched the buttons of the office phone.

"Please Edna, I need someone who can fill in who knows what they are doing. It's just three weeks. I won't ask again." Gwen had heard him.

"Don't lie, Pastor. It's unbecoming in a minister. I know you will ask again if in another jam, and that's okay. The person you have to convince is my husband. He's been waiting for me to retire so we can get away from the snow each winter," Gwen heard Edna's voice come over the speaker phone. Pastor Joe had fumbled to turn off the speaker and looked over at Gwen. "You owe me," he said as he put his hand over the receiver of the phone while Edna gave the phone to her husband.

"There's still plenty of winter left after January. February and March are the worst months." Gwen heard Pastor Joe say. "Yes, I still have that box of Cuban cigars. They're yours if you want them."

Gwen heard Pastor Joe say it was all set before hanging up.

"Thank you, Pastor. You won't regret it," she said as she gave him a hug and rushed out of his office.

That had been the final piece that needed to fall into place.

Chapter 10

Gwen had not been big on attending church in the past. She had attended as a girl because that was what her family did. Every Sunday her mom had dressed all of her kids up and paraded them through the church to the front row, as befitting the family of an important doctor in town. Some Sundays her dad joined them, others he didn't as his work took him away from family on Sundays, that and the occasional golf game.

"With hospital bigwigs," he had always told her mother. Now her dad was one of those bigwigs. He still golfed on Sundays.

Gwen knew something was seriously wrong when her mother stopped going to church while Gwen was in high school. She had insisted Gwen go in her place. Some Sundays Gwen went with her dad. Other Sundays she went alone. She didn't mind. She could sit with Marcie and her dad, or other friends from school. Sometimes Marcie's dad would invite her over for cinnamon rolls after church. Gwen would feel a pull between going with her best friend or going home to check on her mom. When her mom was having a good morning, Gwen accepted the invitation, relishing the gooey rolls and the conversation.

Marcie had stopped going to church when she went away to college. Gwen wasn't sure why she continued to attend. Maybe it was just a habit. Maybe it was the chance to get out of her home and be with all of those "normal" families at church. Whatever the reason, Gwen still attended – not every Sunday, but now and then. She wasn't exactly on good terms with God, but she wasn't on bad terms either. She had long since given up on praying for her mom to be better. Nothing worked, not even prayer. Her mom continued to spiral down a dark staircase that she didn't understand.

Gwen liked Pastor Joe well enough, though she rarely paid attention to his sermons. She enjoyed the ritual of the Lutheran service, the unchanging nature of the ceremony. It gave her a sense of stability and peace she didn't find at home. Yes, it was quiet at home, but it was a brooding quiet, not a peaceful quiet, a quiet filled with dark thoughts as Gwen thought to avoid the clutches of her mother's depression. She stayed busy, running away from home at every opportunity, if only to escape on Sunday for a one-hour service. Marcie hadn't understood why Gwen went to church, especially since she didn't have to.

"It's not so bad, and Pastor Joe's not so bad. I like it." Since starting to work at the church, Gwen had started attending every Sunday. She helped out in Sunday school classes, preferring the youngest. The little kids were fun and took her mind off of problems at home.

Through Ava, Gwen got involved at the dance studio. Ava recruited her assistance with costumes for the Christmas recital.

"I just need an extra pair of hands to make sure the costumes are in place before we release the dancers onto the stage."

"That I can do," Gwen agreed.

"You're the new secretary at St. Luke's," a young voice sounded behind her. Gwen turned around from adjusting the wings of a small fairy and saw Ashley Reese. She knew the family from church.

"Yes, I am."

"I liked the other secretary better – Marcie."

"I like Marcie better too," Gwen told her. Ashley turned around and walked back to await her turn on stage, not saying another word.

"Don't worry about her," Chloe told her. "She's blunt that way. Gets it from her aunt. Thank you for helping out. I'm Chloe. I run the dance studio." Chloe extended her hand to Gwen.

"I thought Kathleen ran the studio."

"She's the executive director of the Center for the Arts, but I take care of the dance studio." Gwen had been surprised at this. Chloe was so young to be in charge of a dance studio. She looked to be not much older than her. At the reception after the recital, Gwen saw her chasing after a toddler. That made her older in Gwen's estimation, but not by much.

"You're young to be in charge of a dance studio, aren't you?" Gwen asked her after she caught up with the toddler.

"I'm older than I look, or so I've been told. It's a good characteristic for a dancer, though not necessarily for running a business. People don't always take me seriously. That's where Kathleen comes in. Everyone takes her seriously." Chloe nodded in Kathleen's direction while holding the squirming toddler.

"What did you do before running the dance studio?"

"I was a dancer on Broadway, so to speak."

"Really?"

"It's not how it sounds." Chloe shook her head to dispel any illusions about her glamorous life. "I only danced in the chorus for a few productions. No big deal. Most of the time I lived the unglamorous life of a waitress in order to pay the bills."

"Do you miss it?"

"Sometimes. What do you do?" Chloe bounced the toddler on her hip.

"I'm a theater major."

"Oh, so you've got the acting bug? What do you hope to do with your degree?"

"Don't know yet. Guess I haven't thought that far. I just like theater, especially costuming. Something will come up."

"I still have a few connections in New York, if you decide you want to go there." Chloe placed the toddler down, holding her hand until she broke loose and ran after another child. "Got to go," Chloe excused herself, ran after the little girl and swooped her up into her arms while the little girl bubbled over with giggles.

"New York," Gwen thought to herself. Could it be possible?

Chapter 11

"Another successful recital," Chloe commented to Kathleen as they prepared to lock up.

"Yeah, it was," Kathleen sat down in one of the chairs that had been set up in the hall for the recital.

"Something wrong?" Chloe sat down next to Kathleen. Esther and Peter had taken Mary off of her hands and taken her home so she didn't miss her bed time.

"Just thinking." Chloe waited for Kathleen to continue. "I'm wondering how my life got here. If you had told me twenty years ago that I would end up back in Cascade Falls running a dance studio, I would have laughed first, then maybe pummeled you."

"What did you want to do?"

"You know," Kathleen pursed her lips and thought. "I don't think I ever planned anything. I just wanted to get out of Cascade Falls and I wanted to have fun. I don't remember ever thinking much beyond that. Hmmm," Kathleen shook her head. "Can you imagine that? I never had any direction. I've just kind of drifted. At least, I didn't have any direction until I came home and became friends with Joy. You never knew Joy," Kathleen sighed. "She was special. She hadn't liked me in high school and I didn't blame her. I don't know that I liked myself much back then. I hadn't paid any attention to Joy. She was just my little brother's girlfriend. But when I came back, during her illness, we became friends, an unlikely friendship."

Kathleen looked away as she continued. "I had come back to be with my boys. That had been the only plan I had. And then Joy left me this building. She told me I needed a purpose in life. My purpose became preserving this building for Joy's sake. But now, the building is on a firm financial footing, at least for a non-profit. My boys are away at college and essentially on their own, and I'm wondering, is this all there is? One Christmas recital after another? A spring recital? Struggling to keep the books in the black?"

"You thinking about leaving?"

"I don't know what I'm thinking. I've preserved Joy's legacy, maybe it's time I figure out what I really want to do with what remains of my life. I've got you to run the dance studio. My mom could easily take over my position as executive director, then I could ..."

"Do what? What do you want to do?"

"I don't know. Maybe go to New York. It seems like that's all anyone talks about. You and Letty." Letty had run the dance studio before Chloe. She was currently in New York dancing with Alvin Ailey II. "Maybe it's time I see what that's all about."

"And then what?"

"I don't know yet. I guess I'll figure it out as I go along."

"Isn't that what got you into trouble? Drifting without a plan?"

"No, this is different. I was young back then, didn't know anything."

"Is this about your break-up with Pastor Joe?"

"No, not at all. That was inevitable. It was just a temporary relationship. One to fill in the gap while I figured out what I wanted."

"You haven't figured it out yet? I thought by the time I hit your age, I'd have it all figured out."

"I thought that too when I was your age, if I thought about it all. I haven't got it figured out, but I will, eventually." At that Kathleen stood up. "Time to get home. We can take care of moving the chairs tomorrow. You've got a baby to get home to."

"And what do you have?"

"I'm working on that," Kathleen said, grabbed her coat and walked with Chloe to the door of the room where she turned out the lights.

Chapter 12

The weeks up to Christmas were packed, as much as they could be for Laura. Gwen had finals to take, plus the play and all of the other volunteer activities she had signed up for. Laura, in anticipation of Christmas with three of her children home was busy making lists of things for Gwen to do, adding to Gwen's workload. She was pushing herself to have some feeling of excitement over the coming holiday. Pleasant feelings were elusive in her current state. She was pushing through the unpleasant feelings and the numbness to get to something better, whatever that might be. She even found the energy to do some Christmas shopping and to supervise the putting up of the tree and give other directions. Gwen was her obedient slave, trying to help her mom create the holiday of her dreams.

Walter was busy calling her two oldest children, leaving voice messages that weren't returned, text messages that remained unanswered. They had not said they were coming home, just that they would try. That was enough for her.

"Of course, they're coming. Why wouldn't they?"

"They are both very busy, Laura. They have their own lives to live. Elizabeth has her husband to consider, Doug his job and his girlfriend," Walter explained.

"They said they would try. I'm sure they will make it. I just wish Clayton could come too."

"I just don't want to see you set yourself up to be disappointed."

"It's Christmas. Christmas is all about disappointments. Kids don't get the toys they want. Mothers don't get the picture-perfect Christmas they want. Don't you think I can deal with that? I will not allow myself to go through life with such low expectations. They will come."

"But if they don't, we can still have a good Christmas, just us and Gwen. Isn't that enough?"

Laura refused to acknowledge what he had said. "They will come."

Walter was at his wits' end trying to get his kids to respond to his calls. They had talked over Thanksgiving weekend but since then he had no response.

"You can't force your kids to call, not once they are on their own," one of his colleagues said when he explained the situation. "Sometimes you just have to let them come to you, in their own time, in their own way."

"You try telling their mother that. Laura is still so fragile. I'm afraid of what another setback could mean. She has her heart set on this Dicken's Christmas with all of the family."

"And Tiny Tim too," Brendan joked.

"Yes, Tiny Tim too. God bless us everyone."

"I'll pray for you, man. I don't know what it is to deal with a wife in her state, but I do know about adult kids who don't return calls. It's hard. That's all I can say."

No, Brendan didn't know what it was to live with Laura. He did know about her depressive episodes and stints in the hospital. How could he keep it a secret? It was a fairly large hospital, the only one in the city, but it functioned like a large extended family, a not so healthy one at times. Everyone thought they knew everyone else's business. At least that was how it appeared to Walter.

No, they didn't know the half of what it was like to live with Laura, or they wouldn't look at him with accusatory frowns when he stayed late or offered to take other doctor's shifts so they could be home with their loved ones. Who knew when he would need the favor in return, he had told himself, when he would have a family situation requiring him to take time off. It hadn't happened yet, but when it did, he would have weeks' worth of favors to cash in. Even during Laura's hospital stays, he had not taken time off. What for? He could visit her on his breaks, then be back at work. And when she came home, Gwen was there to help out. No, when Gwen was gone that's when he would step up, he told himself.

Walter was well aware of why his kids didn't want to come home.

"How's Mom," Betsy had asked him in her own inimitable, cagey way. He could hear the subtext.

"Today was a better day. She would really love to see you. Do you want to talk to her?"

"Not right now, Daddy. Clark is waiting dinner for me. Give her my love, and Gwen too." Walter could hear the relief in her voice from a thousand miles away when she hung up the phone. He could hear it even though they were no longer connected by airwaves. Then, her familial obligations fulfilled, she could return to her own family, her husband Clark and his family. He could hear it in her voice even without speaking.

Douglas wasn't much better.

"You know, you were always her golden boy, her number one son," Walter had urged.

"Really, what about Clay?"

"Come on, Doug. You know how she shines whenever you're around."

"I know, Dad. Look – I'll let you know. Right now, Jocelyn is calling me. I've got to go." But Douglas hadn't let him know. Jocelyn was his girlfriend. She had two sons from a previous marriage. It seemed Douglas had a ready-made family. What did he need with them? If only they were still dependent on him for money, he thought. Then they would come around. They would have to return his calls. What will Gwen do once she, too, is on her own? Will she abandon them too?

Gwen, of the four of them, had it the hardest, he knew. Being the youngest, the one left at home, she bore the brunt of her mother's downhill slide into depression. Their oldest had had more time with the fun mom, with the woman he had married. She had been so full of life back then. He didn't know exactly what had happened, what had caused the first depressive episode. They say it is partially genetic, runs in families. He didn't have to look very far to find evidence for this. There was a history of suicide in her family background, an uncle, a grandfather, great grandfather. Where the men completed suicide, the women were likely to suffer for years with their "trouble." Or be sent away to an asylum. Laura's grandmother had received electric shock therapy after a severe case of post-partum depression. That was back before it was the painless procedure it is today, back in the infancy of psychiatry.

"There is still so much we don't know about the human brain," he had muttered to himself as he had sought out information to help his wife. After the birth of their third child, Elizabeth, Laura had experienced a mild form of post-partum depression. When the normal low feelings that come with the physical exhaustion of childbirth had not abated with rest, her doctor had proscribed a mild anti-depressant. That seemed to do the trick as Laura was soon back to her old self, ordering him around and organizing their life, providing strong structures and exercising control over their children to the extent that anyone can control a baby. She was the model wife and mother, a great hostess to the dinner guests from work that he invited over, a sought-after guest for social gatherings. She lit up the room wherever she went. Yes, there were hints of trouble, but only hints and so easily ignored.

She had another bout with post-partum depression after Gwen was born. Gwen had not been planned. Laura had Clayton, Douglas and Elizabeth into grade school and had started working as a secretary at a local law firm. She had a knack for it and loved the work. She was a born organizer. After only a year she had advanced to office manager.

"See who else is on the upward track," she had told him the night she got the promotion, putting the kids to bed early then greeting him at the door with a bottle of champagne. Walter had been less than enthusiastic, he remembered.

"This won't affect your ability to take care of the kids or the house, will it? Because you know we don't need the money. Now that

I'm out of med school and working at the hospital, we'll be able to pay off my student loans in no time."

"No, silly, it's not about money. It's about me, doing something more with my time besides raising kids." She had wrapped her arms around him and kissed him. "Be happy for me," she had insisted. "And now, let's open this champagne." She had handed him the bottle to open and poured their glasses with glee, allowing the bubbles to overflow and spill onto the counter.

"Don't worry. We can afford some spilled champagne," she had laughed. Her laughter had been infectious. It caught you unaware and tickled you on the inside so that you couldn't keep from joining in no matter how you resisted. He had loved her laugh back then, missed it now.

Then she had become pregnant with Gwen. She wasn't going to quit work, insisted that plenty of other mothers managed to work outside the home, even with a newborn, and she was going to do so too.

"We'll just have to find a good day care or hire a nanny," she had told him. But then the post-partum depression set in and she quit her job and never looked back until it was too late to go back. The position had been filled.

"But if we get another opening, we will call you. We would love to have you back."

It had been a temporary setback. Laura had appeared content being at home with the baby. She had fired the part-time nanny they had hired to help with the baby during her depression and she had set about being a stay-at-home mom until Gwen started a local pre-school program at three. Laura had gotten another secretarial job, part-time, to fit Gwen's pre-school schedule, this time at an insurance agency. Again, she learned the ropes quickly and was offered full-time work. Laura had quit the job abruptly when her boss had grabbed her behind and made suggestive comments about working late.

Walter had come home late, per his usual, and listened to her complaints.

"So quit," he had told her.

"I already have."

"Good, what do we have to eat? I'm exhausted."

Laura had looked at him and said, "Don't you care that that man assaulted your wife?"

"I do care, but what can I do about it? It's over. Why don't you just stay home with the kids? Do you know how many other wives would jump at the chance to not have to work outside the home?"

Laura had stormed off to bed, leaving him to fix his own dinner. But that was the end of Laura's working career, though she often talked about those days to Gwen and anyone else who would listen.

"You know your mother was a great secretary. I used to work for one of the biggest law offices in Philadelphia." Each time she talked about it the firm grew larger and so did she in her own self-importance.

Laura had thought about going back to work once Gwen started school full-time, but then Walter had gotten the new position at the hospital in Cascade Falls. Once they were settled in she had considered looking for a job or even going back to school. She did have a job for a short while. He didn't remember what had happened with that position. Guess he had been too busy at the hospital. Then she had talked about going to school. She hadn't been sure what she would study, said it just seemed like a good idea. She had only had two years of college before dropping out because she was pregnant with Douglas. Those had been hard years, but good ones. There had been little money available while he had gone to med school and then Clayton had been born, followed by Elizabeth. They had had to scrimp to get by, and yet, in retrospect, they were some of the best years of their life together.

Walter wasn't sure exactly when the spiral down had started. Had it started after the move? Or were the seeds already present under the surface waiting for the right stressor to bring it to light? Perhaps the move had been the precipitating event. Perhaps the stress of leaving her hometown, where she had been raised, where she still had family, had set in motion this disorder that had been lying dormant for years. He didn't know if that was what did it. He just wanted his wife back.

It was no secret, his situation at home. There were many sympathetic nurses who were all too willing to provide comfort if he had been willing to accept it. He had secretaries that had indicated as much too. Those he shipped back to the secretarial pool to try their luck with another doctor. He had been tempted, yes, severely so. But he had resisted, burying himself even deeper in his work. Even though he had not given into temptation, he had not been the stellar husband or father. Was it any wonder his kids didn't return his calls? It was every bit as much his fault as it was Laura's. It was just more convenient to blame Laura.

And now he feared he would lose Gwen as well if he didn't do something. But he didn't know what.

Chapter 13

Christmas Eve arrived with still no word back from his two children. Laura remained firm in her belief that they would come. Walter prepared Laura for the worst.

"Should I call? Maybe they would answer me?" Gwen suggested.

"I guess it won't hurt to try," Walter agreed.

"Hey, little sis, what's up?" Gwen looked at her dad in surprise when she got through to Doug right away.

"Merry Christmas. I'm checking. You never got back to Dad. Are you and Jocelyn coming?"

"Oh, hey, we can't make it. I never told Dad we would. I just told him I would see. I'm sorry. Jocelyn has her two boys. We're having Christmas here with them. She couldn't leave them at Christmas."

"Bring them with you."

"Can't. They have to be at their dad's tomorrow for Christmas. But thanks for the invite. Besides it's too late to get tickets and the drive ..."

'Yeah, I know."

"Hey, it was good talking to you. Call again sometime. And tell Mom and Dad I said Merry Christmas."

"He's not coming," Gwen told her dad when she hung up.

"Try Elizabeth." Gwen put the phone on speaker.

"Hey, it's Betsy. I can't come to the phone right now. You know what to do."

"Hi Betsy. It's me, Gwen. I'm just calling to ..."

"Gwen," Gwen heard an actual voice on the phone. "How are you? You never call."

"Well, I've been busy."

"Tell me about it."

"Are you and Clark coming for Christmas?"

"I thought I had told Dad."

"No, you didn't." Gwen looked over at her dad who shook his head no.

"No, I'm sure I did. We can't make it. Got big plans with Clark's family. It's a big deal for them. I couldn't disappoint them but tell Mom and Dad I said Merry Christmas."

"You could call them yourself."

"Look, I've gotta run, but it was good talking to you, sis. Call again."

"Sure," Gwen said as the phone clicked off. "I guess we know now."

"We know, but how do we tell your mom?"

"How do you tell me what?" Laura walked into the kitchen where they had been reconnoitering.

"Tell you how beautiful you look," Walter got up and kissed her. She was dressed for the Christmas Eve service.

"Cut the crap, Walter. What were you two talking about?"

Walter was surprised by the clarity in his wife's voice. He hadn't heard that for a long time. He looked over at Gwen before responding.

"Douglas and Elizabeth aren't coming. Gwen just talked to them."

"Oh," Laura paused a moment then said. "Well, you told me not to get my hopes up, that they hadn't said that they were coming, just that they would think about it. We don't have to let that ruin our night." She paused and looked at them. "You aren't going to church dressed like that are you?"

Gwen and her dad exchanged glances.

"No, Mom. It won't take me long to get ready."

"Me, too, Laura." Both started for the stairs. Walter stopped, turned around and said. "I'm glad you are taking this so well."

"You know I'm not porcelain ready to break. I'm stronger than you realize."

Walter shook his head then proceeded upstairs to get ready for church, following behind Gwen. Walter looked back and saw Laura sitting at the kitchen table.

"All I wanted was one Christmas together as a family again. I guess I can't have even that." Walter heard her mutter as her face took on a look of resolution.

"What, Laura? Did you say something? You sure you're okay?"

"I'm fine, Walter. Now get ready," Laura smiled and sent him on his way.

Chapter 14

Gwen didn't remember when she had enjoyed a Christmas service so much. Her mom was acting like her old self, smiling, talking to others. Gwen stayed in the back of church, helping the kids with their costumes until it was time for them to come forward. Then she slipped into the pew next to her mom. Being a part of the service made it more meaningful. She looked around the crowded church till she saw Marcie sitting with her dad, caught her eye and smiled. Marcie looked at her sitting next to her mom and mouthed, OMG! Gwen just smiled all the brighter. Marcie was aware of all the drama around the holiday, wondering whether her brother and sister would show up, wondering how her mom would take it when they didn't. It appeared that everything had worked out after all.

Gwen found Marcie after the service. "Merry Christmas," she said as they hugged. Then she hugged Marcie's dad. "You are coming over for Christmas dinner, aren't you?"

"Wouldn't miss it," Henry said for both of them. Gwen's parents came up behind her and there were more hugs.

"You look wonderful, Laura," Henry told her.

"Thank you. It was a beautiful service."

"Are your other kids coming home?" Henry asked as Marcie kicked him in the shin.

"No, they aren't going to make it. It will just be us tomorrow," Walter said.

"All the more food for us," Henry tried to make light of his faux pas. "See you tomorrow then."

Marcie scolded him all the way home. "I told you not to say anything."

"I'm sorry, sweetie. It just slipped out."

The reminder about Douglas and Elizabeth didn't put a shadow on their mom's mood. She continued to be her old self through dinner and drinks.

Neither Gwen nor her dad thought anything of it when Laura excused herself.

"Don't you want to watch 'It's a Wonderful Life' with us? It's a tradition," her dad coaxed.

"All I want to do right now is soak in a hot tub," her mom said.

"Okay, Mom, but join us afterwards," Gwen said.

"Sure thing, dear. Merry Christmas." Laura gave her husband and her daughter a kiss and hug before going upstairs.

"That went surprisingly well," Walter said as they cleared away the plates from the table.

"Yeah, I think Mom may finally be on the mend." Gwen joined him in the kitchen. Upstairs they could hear water running.

"Almost too well," her dad said. Something wasn't right. It wasn't like Laura to take disappointment so well.

"Maybe she's getting better," Gwen assured her dad.

"Or maybe ..." Walter took off up the stairs.

"Dad, what's the matter?" Gwen called after him.

"Laura," Walter called out his wife's name as he entered their bedroom. He didn't want to startle her. "Laura," he called again. The water was no longer running.

"Laura?" he said as he opened the door to the master bathroom. He saw Laura's robe in a pile on the floor and looked at the bathtub. The water was red with blood. Laura's head was hanging lifeless to one side.

"Gwen, call 911," he yelled downstairs as he rushed to his wife. He pulled her out of the water, grabbed for the white towels and wrapped them around her wrists while crying softly. "Laura, Laura, why did you do this?"

"What Dad?" Gwen called from downstairs. When he didn't answer she started up the stairs.

"What Dad?" she yelled again.

"Call 911. Tell them it's a medical emergency."

"What?" Gwen said in disbelief, going into her parents' bedroom.

"Call 911. Gwen, don't come in here. It's your mother," Walter's voice broke as he said this. "Call 911."

Gwen stood where she was for a moment as she realized what had happened. She pulled out her phone and dialed 911.

"State the nature of the emergency," a calm voice asked.

How could she be so calm, Gwen wondered as her own pulse was racing.

"It's my mom. She tried to kill herself." Gwen didn't know how she got the words out. She didn't recognize her own voice as she said the words. Who was it talking about suicide? It was another person, another girl named Gwen. It wasn't her, wasn't her mother.

"Give me your address. I'll send someone right away."

Chapter 15

Gwen didn't know how she got to the hospital. Her dad had ridden in the ambulance with her mom. How did she get here? Did she drive? Just then a police officer gave her a cup of coffee.

"Is there anyone I can call for you?" he asked.

"No, I mean, I have a friend, but I can call her. How did I get here?"

"Don't you remember? You rode with us in the squad car. We followed the ambulance."

"Is my mother okay?"

"You'll have to ask the doctor that. Are you sure you're okay?"

"I am, will be. I'll call my friend." The first cop looked over at his partner.

"Come on. We've got to go," his partner said.

"I hate to leave her like this."

"We'll take care of her till her friend comes," the ER nurse told him. "Go ahead. We've got this. You've done your part."

The officer glanced back at Gwen before leaving. She was on her phone but looked up, saw him and nodded an acknowledgment and sent him on his way.

"Marcie?" Gwen's voice shook as she spoke.

"Hey there. I didn't expect to hear from you tonight."

"Marcie," Gwen said again.

"What's wrong?" Marcie's voice became serious.

"I'm at the hospital."

"Gwen, are you all right?" Marcie asked.

"It's my mom."

"Is she all right?"

"I don't know. I think she may be dead. My dad's with her. Can you come?"

"I'll be right there." Marcie hung up the phone.

"What's wrong?" her dad asked.

"Gwen's mom is at the hospital. I've got to go."

"Not alone. Not on Christmas Eve. I'll go with you." Henry turned off the TV, shutting off the sounds of "It's a Wonderful Life".

Henry drove as fast as he could. Christmas songs were playing on the radio as he drove, taking on a macabre aspect in light of what had happened. Marcie reached over and turned the radio off.

"Thank you," was all her dad said. They rode the rest of the way in silence. Her dad dropped her off at the emergency room door while he parked the car. Marcie ran into the waiting room and sought out her friend. Gwen's tall frame looked shrunken, sitting alone and huddled in the metal chair. Marcie rushed to her and hugged her.

"Do you know anything yet?"

"No, I think they are still working on her." Gwen started to cry. "Marcie, remember what I said last summer, how sometimes I wished she would just die. I didn't mean it."

"I know you didn't mean it. You were just upset."

"But now if she dies, how could I live with myself. It's all my fault."

"It's not your fault. Your mom will be okay. We've been through this before. She pulled through before. She'll pull through again."

"But this time is different."

"How?"

"She was so determined. It was like, she had gathered up all her energy for this one last night. Her last hurray ... Am I making any sense?"

"Sure you are, sweetie," Marcie said as her dad joined them.

"Any word?" Henry asked.

"No, we're still waiting," Gwen said.

"I'm going to call Pastor Joe," Henry said.

"On Christmas Eve?" Marcie asked.

"He'll want to know. Maybe he can be some help." Henry walked away from them to place the call. "He's on his way," he said when he came back.

Joe had been relaxing with his daughters, playing Scrabble, when his phone rang.

"Let it go to voice mail, Dad," Stephanie said. "What can be so important that they have to call on Christmas Eve?" Stephanie and Michelle were used to holidays being interrupted by church emergences. Joe knew that didn't make it any easier.

"But if it's important enough that they call on Christmas Eve, maybe you better take the call," Michelle said.

Joe looked at both of them. Sometimes he hated his job and how it pulled him away from his family. How many more Christmases would be ruined by church emergencies?

"Go on, Dad. Answer it. Maybe it's nothing, but better to know," Michelle said.

Joe answered the phone, his face growing increasingly serious as the call went on.

"Okay," he said. "I'll be right there."

"What is it, Dad?" Stephanie asked.

"You know I can't tell you. It's serious though. I have to go."

"Okay, Dad. We'll leave the light on for you," Michelle said.

Joe found the small group huddled together in the waiting room. "Any word yet?"

"Yes," Henry stepped forward. "They think she's going to make it. She lost a lot of blood, but fortunately Walter was able to stop the bleeding in time. She's getting a transfusion now. Gwen's dad was just out here. He went back to check on her again."

Gwen was crying as Marcie held her. "Why does this keep happening?" she asked. Joe sat down next to her.

"Your mother is in so much pain, pain that we can't see. Sometimes when someone is in pain, they just see no other way out," Joe said.

"I can't believe she did this. And on Christmas Eve," Gwen said. Joe just sat with them.

Chapter 16

Gwen spent the night at Marcie's. Walter stayed overnight with Laura. He was sleeping in the chair by her bed but woke quickly when he heard her moan.

"I'm here," he took her hand in his and gently called her name. "Laura."

"Why didn't you let me die?" Laura didn't open her eyes.

"I love you."

"If you loved me you would have let me go."

Walter didn't know what to say to that. All of his training, his years as a physician, he had been taught to save life. It was instinctual.

"Laura, why? Why Christmas Eve? Was it just because Elizabeth and Douglas didn't come? Aren't Gwen and I enough? Aren't I enough?"

"It wasn't about Elizabeth and Douglas. It's not about you. I was going to do it anyway. I just wanted to see them one last time. This just moved up the timeline. I just want to escape this misery. Let me go," she pleaded with him then fell back into a restless sleep.

Where was she? Not heaven. Could this be hell? She had already been living her own hell on earth. Why not continue in the next life? Groggy. Head fog. Can hardly move. Who was that sitting next to her bed? Was it her pastor? Or someone else? She mumbled something. Can't remember what. Was this the emergency room? Or some other room, she didn't know?

Why was she still alive? Why was she here? She slipped in and out of a drug-induced sleep.

Laura had been aware of her daughter's presence for a brief moment that the night. Gwen had taken her hand and kissed her on the forehead.

"I love you, Mom," Gwen had said.

Laura mumbled a reply. "Love you too."

"She needs her sleep," the nurse had said as she escorted her out.

Then Pastor Joe was there. She barely acknowledged his presence, closing her eyes as he approached the bed.

"What are you doing here?" she whispered. "If you've come to give me cheap absolution, I don't want it. I'll take my lumps when I meet my maker."

"No, I just came to pray." Joe took her hand and quietly prayed by her bedside before leaving.

Her mother was asleep the next day when Gwen came to visit.

"What she needs right now is rest and twenty-four-hour supervision. We'll take care of that. You need to go home and get some rest yourself," the doctor told her and her dad. "Once she's stronger we'll move her to the psych ward. She's on suicide watch. There's really nothing more you can do."

Henry gave Gwen and her dad a ride home. Marcie hugged Gwen before she left.

"If you need me, call me," she whispered into Gwen's ear as they hugged.

"You are always the first call I make," Gwen told her.

Left alone in the big house, Gwen and her dad didn't know where to start.

"You hungry?" her dad asked.

"No, I had breakfast at Marcie's."

"Okay." Walter started a pot of coffee. "I guess I better go upstairs and clean the mess in the bathroom."

"You don't have to do it now, Dad. Have your coffee first. I'll help."

They sat at the kitchen table while Walter sipped his coffee.

"I want you to know," he put the coffee down and looked directly at Gwen, "this is not your fault."

"I know, Dad."

"But do you believe it?" Gwen didn't answer. "And it's not Betsy or Doug or Clay's fault."

"If only they had come, Mom wouldn't have done this."

"No, that would have just prolonged the inevitable. She told me so last night. She had been planning this for a while, had hidden away a razor blade. She just wanted see them again and Christmas seemed the right excuse to get them to come home."

"But if they had been here, maybe she would have changed her mind. Maybe that would have been enough to get her to want to live."

"We don't know that." Her dad's phone rang. He looked at who it was. "Betsy. Finally returning my call."

"You don't have to answer it right now, Dad. You need some sleep and so do I."

They threw the blood-stained towels away and tried to wash the blood out of the tub and floor.

"It's going to take more than a soapy wet cloth to clean this mess," her dad said. "I'll call someone tomorrow. I'll just use the hall bathroom." Walter closed the door to the bathroom before lying down fully clothed on the bed and falling asleep. Gwen left him there, closing the door behind her as he slept.

Gwen tried to sleep, too, but her brain wouldn't let her. She wandered down into the living room where the tree was still surrounded by presents. What were they going to do with these presents? Maybe they should wait until her mom came home from the hospital, but when would that be? Maybe they could take them to the hospital when her mom was feeling better. Maybe she and her dad should just pack them away for another day. Maybe they would forego Christmas this year.

Chapter 17

"Dad, you forgot to open your present," Stephanie placed a small, wrapped, rectangular box in front of him as he finished breakfast. "Remember, good things come in small packages. That's what you always told us."

"I thought we were opening presents at Grandma's." As soon as breakfast was done they were going to get on the road for the two-hour drive to Joe's parents. They would spend the rest of Christmas day there, then stay over for another day before heading back. Other years his parents had come and stayed with him since he always had the Christmas Eve service, but this year his dad wasn't feeling up to the trip so they had agreed to do the driving. His older brother and wife were going to be there as well.

"No, this one you have to open here. It's from me and Michelle," Stephanie insisted.

"Yeah, come on, Dad. Open it," Michelle added.

What were they up to, Joe wondered as he tore off the paper. He carefully lifted the top of the box, thinking something would pop out at him at any moment. When nothing emerged, he took the top off and pulled back the tissue paper lining. There lay two tickets to the New Year's Eve Gala put on by the hospital each year.

"Thank you for the thought, girls, but in case you haven't noticed, I don't have a date," he said as he pulled the tickets out.

"That's the best part. We've got you a date," Stephanie said.

"What?"

"We've got you a date," Stephanie repeated.

"Yeah, Dad, we figured if we waited for you to ask someone out, we'd both be long gone with kids of our own before you made your move," Michelle added.

"I can find my own dates," he stated.

"Yeah, well how is that working for you?" Stephanie asked.

"This isn't another attempt to get me back together with Scott's mom?" In the past Stephanie and Michelle had "encouraged" the relationship with help from Scott.

"Really, Dad. We know that's just not gonna happen. Time for you to move on. You aren't getting any younger you know," Stephanie said.

"Thanks, Mom." Joe frowned. His mother had said the same thing, repeatedly.

"I just mean ..."

"I know what you mean. So, who is this mystery date?"

"That's the best part. It's a mystery. You don't find out until you pick her up." Michelle grinned. Mystery date had been one of her favorite games as a girl, Joe remembered.

"No way. Either I know who this woman is beforehand or I'm not going."

"I told you he wouldn't buy the mystery part," Stephanie told Michelle. "Don't worry, Dad. You'll like her. She's new to town. And, she's a doctor."

"She helps out at the clinic on Wednesday evenings," Michelle added.

"Do I know her?"

"We told you, she's new to town. And she doesn't attend St. Luke's if that's what you are asking. I think she's Catholic," Stephanie said.

"Hmmm, an interesting choice." Joe liked the fact that she wasn't a church member. That always brought complications. But Catholic? He wondered how that would play out with his congregation. At least she went to church. That might be a nice change.

"What does it matter," Stephanie interrupted his thought pattern. "She's cute and she's single and within your age range."

"What does that mean?"

"It means we don't want a step mother who is our age like Cara from church." Since his divorce, Cara's dad had recently starting dating a twenty-something.

"So, she's fortyish?" Joe turned his hand back and forth.

"More like thirtyish, but a late thirtyish," Stephanie replied.

"I can deal with that."

"Look, Dad. If you want to check her out, just go to the clinic on Wednesday. Make up some excuse. Or go to the hospital. You are certainly there enough. Maybe you'll run into her while she's making her rounds."

"And how did you get her to agree to this?"

"Scott introduced us. Seems she has a daughter our age. Scott met her over Thanksgiving weekend," Stephanie explained.

"Hmmm, the plot thickens. She agreed to this date?"

"Well, she didn't want to at first, but Scott and Alex talked her into it. Look, Dad, if you don't want to do it, that's up to you, but you are going to have to call her and cancel, not us. Here, her name is Julia Hennessey," Stephanie gave her dad Dr. Hennessey's business card. "Don't you think we should be getting ready to go to Grandma's?" she added as she stood up.

Joe was left sitting at the table with tickets in one hand and the business card in the other.

Chapter 18

Walter had gone into work the next day, though originally he had the day off. That left Gwen to take care of putting away the Christmas decorations.

"This is one Christmas that wasn't meant to be," he had said as Marcie showed up to help Gwen. "Thank you for helping," he told Marcie. "I'm just not up to it. Thank you for helping Gwen with this," he repeated before leaving.

"I'd rather keep busy," he told his secretary when he came in. Word about Laura had already spread through the hospital. Walter brusquely pushed aside any words of sympathy. He was abrupt with the hospital staff, but warm and compassionate as he sat at his patient's bedsides. He took time to listen to their stories and give comfort, something he was usually in too much of a hurry to do. The nurses noticed the change. Not that he was ever cold and uncaring. But he had rarely taken the time to sit with his patients as he rushed from room to room, always in a hurry to complete his rounds and get back to his administrative duties. He was still moving quickly between rooms, not looking up as he looked over charts while walking.

He bumped into the new oncologist as he quickened his pace to reach the elevator.

"Oh, I'm sorry, doctor ...?"

"Hennessey." Julia filled in the blank for him.

"Yes, I remember interviewing you for the position."

"I thought only newbies like me had to work the week between Christmas and New Year's." Her eyes sparkled, blue with flecks of grey, as she smiled. Clearly, she didn't know about his wife, Walter thought. It was a relief to talk to someone on staff without sympathy oozing out. He didn't want or need sympathy.

"How are you liking your new position?" Walter hoped he didn't sound as much like a stuffed shirt to her as he did to himself.

"Awesome," Julia smiled. She specialized in treating children's cancer. He had recruited her from St. Jude Children's Hospital with the promise of being in charge of the new oncology unit when the current physician in that position retired next year.

"How can you be so cheerful?" he asked her. "Dealing with all of those cancer patients, especially children?"

"It's Christmas."

"Yes, but you are working in a hospital, treating patients who would rather be anywhere else but here."

"All the more reason why they need someone smiling."

"I guess." They rode the elevator to the sixth floor together. "Are you attending the New Year's Eve fundraiser?" Walter asked.

"I am. I have a date. Can't wait."

"That's good. The money is going towards the new cancer wing," Walter said. "Is that why you are so happy? Your date?"

"No, it's a blind date. My daughter fixed me up. So, no, it's not because of my date. I just think it's an amazing opportunity to meet people. Will you be there?"

Walter stopped to think about that. What was he going to do? He had to put in an appearance. His position required it. But how could he? Laura couldn't attend and it had long since ceased being fun for Gwen after attending two times. Gwen would much rather be with her friends. He was grateful when the elevator door opened, giving him the excuse he needed to leave without answering her question.

"How was work?" Gwen asked her dad as they sat down to the meal she had prepared – grilled cheese sandwiches and tomato soup.

"Work is work," her dad failed to offer more to the conversation.

"And how is Mom?"

"I don't know. They moved her to the psych ward today. We'll see how long she stays there." Gwen could tell her dad didn't want to talk about either his job or her mom.

"I guess I won't be going to Guatemala."

"What are you talking about?" her dad popped his head up from where it had been fixated on his soup, head down and eyes lowered. Gwen figured she had finally gotten his attention.

"How can I go with Mom in the hospital and all? I can't leave you."

"I'll be fine and your mother is in good hands. What good would it do for you to miss your trip?"

"What if you need me?"

"I can handle three weeks by myself. You are going."

"But Dad ..."

"No, it's settled. You've already given up so much for your mother. I can't let you do this."

"Okay." Gwen wasn't sure whether she was relieved or upset. How could she go away now? She would worry the whole time she was gone.

"It will be good for you, help you take your mind off of your mother for a while. What would you do if you were here besides worry? You can worry just as well in Guatemala, and you might even have some fun while there, which is more than I can say about being home with me."

"Thanks, Dad." She did want to go.

"So, do you and Marcie have plans for New Year's?"

"Marcie's going to Nashville to see Bernie. She invited me to come with, but who wants to be a third wheel."

"You wouldn't want to go to the hospital fundraiser with me, would you?"

"Honestly?" Gwen looked over at her dad. Did she dare tell him what she really thought about those stuffy affairs? Her mother had been the one to love them, not her, not once she had her opportunity to attend. "I'd rather not."

"Me neither. How about we stay home and play cards? I'll teach you cribbage."

"Sure, Dad. It's a date."

Chapter 19

Joe had been surprised when called in to consult on Laura Thompson's case.

"We don't ordinarily do this," Dr. Kremer had said after sitting down at the table in the consultation room and making introductions. "Some ministers do more harm than good. We are careful about who has access to our patients and at times have had to restrict clergy visits. However, Laura's family asked that you see her, so we thought we would try something different, include more of a spiritual component to Laura's recovery plan." Sitting with him at the table were Laura's husband, Dr. Thompson, and Dr. Chapman, head of the psych unit.

"So, I would be part of the treatment team?" Joe asked.

"Yes, you have a good reputation within the community for your counseling skills. We try to take a holistic approach to healing, addressing physical, mental, emotional needs of our patients. Sometimes the spiritual needs are neglected. That's where you come in," Dr. Kremer explained.

"As long as you don't practice any voodoo, hocus pocus religion that tells the patient to pray and everything will be better or blames the patient for a lack of faith or a lack of will power," Dr. Chapman jumped in. "I'm not necessarily an advocate of this addition to treatment, but Dr. Kremer is the lead psychiatrist on this case and it's agreeable to Dr. Thompson and the patient, so I'm willing to let them try it."

"That is, if you are willing," Dr. Kremer told Joe. Joe realized he would be under scrutiny during this "probationary" period. If he failed, it would be harder for other ministers to be instrumental in the healing process for their church members. There would be more locked doors.

"What exactly would this entail?" Joe asked.

"Regular weekly visits with the patient and attending the weekly conference when we discuss the patient's treatment and progress as needed. You won't have to attend all of these but are welcome to attend."

How could he fit in yet another commitment? Yet how could he say no? "Okay, I'm in," Joe said.

"Good, we'll put your name on the approved visitor list for Mrs. Thompson. You can start visiting any time you are ready. We'll contact you in regards to the treatment conferences."

"Thank you for doing this," Walter told Joe as they walked out together. "We've tried so many treatment options, different meds, talk therapy, group sessions, electric shock therapy. I'm willing to try anything to help Laura get better. Even God."

"Most people I deal with, God is their first line of defense."

"Well, most people you deal with are not doctors. We are men and women of science. But I'll try anything."

Joe had been distracted by the meeting in the psych unit that was located in an adjoining building to the hospital. He had been so distracted that while on his way back to the main hospital to visit a church member he started to walk through the electronic outside door without asking who had pushed the button. He collided with Dr. Hennessey causing her to drop her brief case, which briefcase opened, spilling its contents on the wet ground.

"I'm so sorry," Joe said as he bent over to pick up the papers before they blew away.

"That's okay. I should have been watching," Julia said as she scrambled after the papers as well.

Joe looked up into the eyes of the doctor, "Can I buy you a coffee to make it up to you?" This truly was a day of surprises. He had never done that before, ask a total stranger out for coffee, even one as pretty as this one. He didn't even know if she were single.

Her face lit up in a smile, "Sure, that would be awesome."

"You aren't angry at me for knocking your papers on the ground?"

"Should I be? If I had been paying attention I wouldn't have bumped into you."

Now, this was different, Joe thought to himself. Most women he knew would have bit his head off and blamed him, at least Kathleen would have.

"I'm Joe," he reached over to shake her hand.

"And I'm Julia. I'm new to town."

"I didn't think I recognized you. I would have remembered you if I had." Julia's blond hair was pulled back in a simple pony tail. Bangs hid a high forehead, and her smile ... Joe was intrigued.

"How about that coffee?" Joe asked.

"Actually, I was just on my way home. Maybe another time."

"And I was just about to visit a church member," Joe admitted.

"You aren't Pastor Joe Michaels, the minister from the Lutheran church, are you?"

"Yes, I am. And you are?"

"That's awesome. I'm your date for New Year's Eve. Julia Hennessey. When my daughter tried to set me up with a minister, I was hesitant, but I figured I needed a date and it was for a good cause, so what the hell. Ooops, sorry there."

"No need to be, sorry that is."

"Oh, I'm not at all, sorry about the date that is." Joe loved the easy way she laughed. So different from ... but no, better not to compare.

"So, I guess I'll see you New Year's Eve," Joe said.

"It will be epic," Julia replied.

Chapter 20

Where was she now? Laura looked around the bare room. Crap. Was she back in the psych unit? The place she had sworn she would never return to? Crap. How did she end up here? What did she remember?

Christmas Eve. It was all supposed to be over on Christmas Eve. She was going to be done with this life. She had said goodbye in her own fashion. Went to services with her family, what family she had. What had gone wrong?

Damn. Walter. It must have been him. He must have saved her. Why? Why couldn't he have let her go? What good was she? What good was living? She would be better off dead. Her family would be better off without her. Pressure to end her life pushed against her brain till it hurt. She had to end this pain. She looked around the room. Nothing. Crap.

She was in an eight-by-ten-foot room, bed close to the floor, nothing on the walls. A fluorescent light was inlaid into the ceiling. No fixture someone could try to hang from. No means of taking sheets from your bed and using them. She had been stripped down to the bare essentials. No clothes but a hospital gown to wear. No friendly reminders of who she was or the home or life she had led outside of the confines of this room. That was okay. She wouldn't have welcomed the reminders. She didn't want any reminders of the life outside of these four walls. Wanted to forget it all, wrap herself in a numb shell where she could crawl away and never return.

Damn, God, why didn't you let me die?

She would have to be smarter this time. She would make sure when she left this time she would never come back. She would make a deal with the devil if she had to. God wasn't helping. Maybe Satan would.

Part of her recoiled at the thought. Was she really that bad off? She wasn't so sure about God right then, but she figured she would rather take her chances with God than the devil. Still, the thought, once allowed, began to take up residence in her brain. Was this her escape valve? Her only way out? She didn't know.

Joe set up a regular time to visit Laura in the psych unit after his initial visit with her in the emergency room and the meeting with her psychiatrist. He was surprised at what he found when he visited her that week between Christmas and New Year's.

She was not the Laura he remembered. That Laura had never left home without her hair done and make-up. She always dressed meticulously. Who was this woman he was visiting? But a vapor of the woman he had known, a vapor of the elegant spirit he remembered and admired. How could she have sunk so low? And how could he have gone so long without visiting this church member? Guilt popped up only to be suppressed in order to attend to the situation at hand. He made a mental note. He would deal with his guilt later.

She was but a vapor and looked like she could blow away, slip away to some faraway place at the least wrong move. Dear God, how was he to deal with this? There was a sense of evil present in the room, something he had only experienced once before, during his seminary training. He had been doing a unit of CPE, clinical pastoral education, at a prison psych unit. It had been the hardest three months of his training. Each day he had come home and felt the need to shower and immerse himself in prayer.

There was a shadowy presence in Laura's room. It evaporated at his approach, but Joe felt it wasn't far gone. It was just awaiting an opportunity to pounce.

Joe squatted next to Laura's bed. There was no chair available in the room. He made a mental note to ask about bringing in a chair the next time he visited.

"Laura, how are you?" Joe searched her face for any indication of how to proceed. Laura lay unresponsive on her bed, staring at the ceiling.

"Laura?" he asked again.

Laura looked at him. Had he ever seen such a depth of sadness? And an emptiness that was frightening.

"Who are you?" Laura asked.

"It's me. Pastor Joe. Remember me? I prayed with you in the hospital emergency room on Christmas Eve."

"Why didn't you just let me die?" Joe didn't respond to this. Every word that came to him seemed just as empty as her eyes. He didn't know how to respond to such a sorrow.

Finally, he stated, "I see your suffering."

Laura grabbed his hand, squeezing it like her life depended on his answer to her. Joe was surprised by the strength in the seemingly emaciated and frail woman.

"What do you know about suffering?" She snarled as she continued to squeeze his hand, then her voice took on a pleading whine. "You've got to get me out of here. Please, get me out of here?"

"You're not well. You have to get better, be stronger, before you leave."

Laura let go of her grip and stared back at the ceiling. "Then what good are you?"

Joe wasn't sure what to do. Was this his cue to leave? He was usually good at catching those cues. No one needed a minister hanging around past his time to leave. Knowing when to leave was an important pastoral tool.

"Did you want me to leave?"

"Whatever." Laura continued to stare at the ceiling.

"Would you like me to pray for you?"

"Whatever you want. What good will it do? I'm all prayed out."

Joe took her hand and prayed quietly. He searched for words he didn't have, trusting God to fill in his lack, not trusting himself with the words out loud.

"Dear God," he prayed quietly, his head lowered. "I don't know how or what to pray for this woman, but you know her needs better than I do, better than she does. I pray that you will give me the words I need, or silence, if that will serve you better. Bless this woman in all of her pain. Relieve her suffering and may I in some small way help her in her struggle."

"Amen," he finally said. Laura had been watching him the whole time. He felt her eyes boring into his scalp as if trying to surgically cut open his brain and discover what was there.

"What did you pray?"

"I prayed that God would relieve your suffering."

"Did you pray for God to get me out of here?"

"Do you want me to pray that?"

"Yes, pray for that."

"Okay." This time Joe spoke his thoughts. "Dear God, I pray that you heal this woman so she can return to her family, in your time and in your way."

"Pray that I never come back to this place."

"And I pray that this time, when she leaves, she will be fully healed and never return. Amen."

Laura seemed satisfied with that prayer. He didn't know why something didn't feel right about the prayer. Perhaps it had something to do with the darkness he had felt when he entered the room. Perhaps Laura meant something different from what he had meant when he prayed that she would never come back. Joe thought he saw a shadow in the corner of the room, one that he had noticed before, one that crept across the room and disappeared. He looked. The shadow was gone. Still, something inside him shivered.

Some demons are not cast out so easily. Some require prayer and fasting. He wondered what he was dealing with. He quietly prayed a prayer of protection for Laura. She had a long way to go.

Chapter 21

"Mom, any plans for New Year's Eve?" Josh asked over their morning coffee.

"As a matter of fact, I have a date," Kathleen answered.

"Yeah, Mom. Who's this new guy you're dating?" Scott asked.

"A local lawyer, Henry Taylor," Kathleen stirred her coffee, waiting fe information to sink in. Imagine her, dating a lawyer.

"Marcie Taylor's dad?" Scott asked.

"Do you know him?" Kathleen asked.

"No, but remember, everybody knows Marcie, or at least used to, from her blog."

"Right. That." Kathleen's claim to fame as the buxom brunette. It had been fun while it had lasted.

"Where are you going?" Josh asked.

"The hospital's New Year's Eve gala, not that it's anyone's business."

"Oh, a formal party. I didn't think you liked getting dressed up," Josh said.

"Shows you how much you know. Even a jaded old woman in her forties, like me, can enjoy dressing up like a princess now and then." It had been Henry's idea. The hospital was one of his biggest clients. There was a lot of money to be made with malpractice lawsuits, on both sides. He usually represented the hospital.

"I thought you were all about protecting the rights of the little guy," Kathleen had said when he had told her.

"You know, hospitals have rights too. They aren't corrupt, money-grubbing businesses that some people make them out to be. They are full of doctors who just want to help people get better and who do their best to care for them. I'm telling you, the majority of lawsuits are not cases of criminal neglect and wrong-doing on the part of the hospital or the doctors involved. Sometimes it's just hurting people wanting to lash out. Sometimes it's greedy people looking for easy money through suing the hospital and hoping for a settlement out of court. I'm telling you, it's not like I'm working for the insurance companies or big pharma."

"Okay, counselor. You don't have to get up on your soap box." Kathleen regretted bringing it up.

Kathleen had agreed to the date before realizing it required formal attire, none of which she possessed.

"Don't worry, Kathleen. I have some formals from weddings I've attended over the years. I'm sure we can find something suitable," Esther had told her when she brought it up while at the dance studio putting away costumes from the Christmas recital.

Kathleen cringed, "Thanks, Mom, but really?"

"Don't worry, Kathleen," Chloe intervened. "There's this great resale store that specializes in prom dresses."

"I'm not going to a prom."

"Yeah, I know the place." Gwen had been helping with the costumes. "Chloe and I can take you there. With the right formal, I can work my magic and transform you into an elegant princess."

"What about my offer? It still stands," Esther said as Chloe and Gwen whirled Kathleen away.

"You mind the studio, Esther. We'll take care of Kathleen," Chloe told her.

Gwen's talk about a princess had worried Kathleen. She wondered what she was getting herself into during the ride to the store but was pleased with the final result as Chloe and Gwen dressed her up like one of the students in a recital.

"It's similar to the ball gowns Michelle Obama wore, but different enough that it doesn't look like you are copying her. Mature and elegant, simple lines," Gwen said as she added some finishing touches to the deep scarlet gown with sequined bodice and flowing skirt.

"Now for your hair. What do you think, up or down?" Gwen asked Chloe.

"Up, of course. Every well-dressed princess wears her hair up."

"I'm not a princess," Kathleen had insisted back then. On the night of the gala though, when she saw herself in the mirror she wondered. She had not attended her high school prom. It just hadn't interested her. Had she missed out on something? She had a calf-length, black cashmere coat, her mom's, to wear over her gown, and heels, not so high to throw her off balance and mess up her ability to dance, but high enough to add the finishing touch.

"You are a bundle of contradictions, Kathleen Anne Reese," her mom said after seeing the finished product.

"What do you mean, Mom?"

"You're as cocky and self-assured as any corporate CEO, running deals. You fit in with those living on the streets, the poor, drug dealers, as well as those with money."

"When I need to."

"But you can also be a lady, as elegant as any princess."

"I guess I'll take that as a compliment." Suddenly Kathleen didn't feel so self-assured. This was a new feeling. Was this how it felt to be uncertain of yourself? She didn't like this feeling. Maybe she should back out of the date.

"I meant it as one," Esther said.

Too late. The doorbell rang and Henry escorted her down the sidewalk.

"You look incredible," Henry told her as he guided her into his car.

"You clean up pretty good, too," Kathleen told him. The new feeling had yet to fade away.

Chapter 22

Julia wore her hair down on her shoulders. She was every bit as comfortable in her simple ivory floor-length gown as she was in her white doctor's jacket. A strap went over her right shoulder, leaving her left shoulder and her arms bare, exposing her flawless skin.

Joe was both in awe and out-of-place beside such a beautiful woman. They walked about the room, looking at auction items for the silent auction, eventually ending up at their table with the other doctors from the oncology unit.

Joe could feel the ripple of comments throughout the room as he escorted his date, even though he could not hear them. He could tell by the looks thrown their way. Looks from single, female church members who had had hopes of latching onto the pastor now that he was available again. Looks from doctors, jealous of the pretty young woman who had landed the plum position of soon-to-be head of the oncology department. And jealous stares from men who envied him his beautiful date. Not that Kathleen had been less than beautiful, just in a different way.

He took out his phone and sent a brief text message to his daughters, "Thank you!"

Then he saw Kathleen come through the door escorted by Marcie Taylor's dad, Henry. He had never seen her look so beautiful, her hair piled on her head, showing an elegant neck. The scarlet of her dress brought out the flush of red on her cheeks from the cold outside. She seemed momentarily ill-at-ease as she scanned the room, out of her comfort zone. He had never known Kathleen to be out of her comfort zone. She had always appeared so self-assured. Was it self-assurance, or false bravado? This slightly shy, insecure Kathleen was a new side to her, one he had never seen. He looked away, lest she catch him staring, but found himself taking side glances at her throughout the dinner, despite the charming dinner companion by his side.

Once the dinner plates had been cleared away, the music started for dancing – ballroom dancing. Joe was pleased to discover that his dancing partner was as natural on the dance floor as she was in every other aspect of her life, a gracious guest who was interested in what other people had to say, friendly, a kind word for everyone. The perfect pastor's wife, Joe caught himself thinking.

"You've done this before," Joe commented as they waltzed.

"Yes, well, being from the south, every debutante knows how to dance. It was not optional but required – a tradition." Joe loved the slight southern drawl that crept into her voice at times.

"I like that tradition. Do you have any other traditions to tell me about?"

"Oh, and I'm an amazing skeet shooter."

"Not something I know anything about. I take it your family has money?"

"Yes, but I hope you won't hold that against me. We can't help who our parents are, can we?" Again with the twang as she smiled up at him.

"No," Joe knew what he wanted to hold against her, but such thoughts weren't appropriate for a pastor.

Joe looked over and saw Kathleen dancing with Henry. She had improved, but still stumbled and struggled against following Henry's lead at times. Not at all like Julia, who slipped into his arms so gracefully and followed the slightest touch of his hand.

Julia excused herself after the dance to go to the "powder room." Joe saw Kathleen heading in the same direction. He raised his eyebrow at the thought of the two of them running into each other, then went over to the bar to get drinks.

"Nice party," Henry commented as he joined Joe in the line for the bar.

"Yes, it is," Joe responded.

"This your first time coming?"

"Yes, what about you?"

"I've been coming for years. Pretty much obligatory when you do business with the hospital."

"My daughters bought tickets for me. It was their Christmas gift. Said I needed to get out more."

"Did they also arrange your date?"

"In fact, they did."

"I don't recognize her. I thought I knew all the doctors in town. She must be the new doctor they've been talking about."

"I'll introduce you," Joe told him.

Even the powder room was fancy in this place, Kathleen thought as she checked her make-up in the sitting area before the stalls and sinks. She sat down on one of the chairs. This had been a mistake, she told herself. She didn't belong here. She looked into her purse for her lipstick. If only she had stuck a reefer into her purse. That would have calmed her down some. But no, someone would have smelt it and reported her and she would have been escorted out by some burly security guard. At least that would have gotten her out of here. Maybe now that Henry had put in his appearance, maybe they could leave. Either that or she could hang out in here all night.

She had seen Joe dancing with that blonde. She didn't recognize her. She wondered where he had found her, then the blonde appeared and went to the mirror to adjust her lipstick.

"Lovely party, isn't it?" the blonde said.

"If you like these things."

"I take it you don't?"

"It's just not really me."

"I'm Julia, by-the-way. And you are?" Kathleen continued to sit and stare at the young woman. Was she for real? How could anyone be so full of goodness and light? She was freakishly like Glinda the good witch. And if Julia was Glinda, that made her the wicked witch of the west. Seemed fitting.

"Kathleen," Kathleen accepted her outreached hand. "Are you for real?"

"Whatever do you mean?"

"How can you be so cheery? It's just a fundraiser for the hospital. I can think of a lot of better ways to have fun."

"Well, I think it's amazing."

"Sure you would." Kathleen continued to sit. If only she had that reefer.

"I guess I better get back to my date."

"You do that."

"Nice meeting you," Julia said.

"Sure, whatever." Kathleen felt like what little bit of excitement she had left about the party was gone, drained away by too much goodness. It seemed Julia was bringing out the bad in her. She couldn't tolerate someone so perky.

Kathleen got up, checked her dress, and headed back into the ballroom. She looked for Henry and saw him talking to Joe and that little witch. Glinda, Julia, whatever. Too late. Henry saw her and motioned for her to join them. There was no slipping back into the bathroom.

"Kathleen, this is Julia," Henry started to introduce them.

"We've already met."

"Yes, in the powder room." Julia laughed. What was so funny, Kathleen wondered.

"Julia's new in town. Maybe we could show her around some time. She's very interested in the Center for the Arts," Henry said.

"Yes, I'm a big supporter of the arts, opera, the symphony," Julia said.

"We are just a little center with a dance studio and an art gallery. It's no big deal," Kathleen said.

"I'm sure it's amazing." Was there any getting away from this woman, Kathleen wondered. And did she always talk in superlatives?

"Sure. Henry, don't we have to get back to our table?"

"Oh, no. Now that the dinner's over we can sit wherever we want."

"Come join us. I'd love to hear more about that awesome dance studio," Julia said.

Kathleen looked at Joe for help, since her own date was clearly oblivious to how uncomfortable she was. Joe shrugged his shoulders and followed after Julia as she wrapped her arm around Kathleen.

There was no escaping Julia after that. She had determined that they would be friends. She prattled on and on about the dance studio and Center for the Arts, asking Kathleen questions, then not waiting for an answer.

"I haven't made a best friend since coming here. I think you would be the perfect candidate," Julia said. Both Henry and Joe laughed at this. Kathleen was actually happy to get back on the dance floor if only to get away from Julia for a while.

At one point they switched. That left Kathleen dancing with Joe.

"So, Julia, she seems nice. You an item?" Kathleen asked.

"Just our first date, but she is nice, very friendly."

"Too friendly. Don't you find that annoying?"

"Why no, I find it refreshing," Joe smiled over at Julia who smiled back.

"When can we leave?" Kathleen asked Henry when rescued from Joe.

"We can't leave before midnight. You don't want to miss the ball drop and champagne, do you? And we have the best view of the fireworks from up here. Much better than being outside in the cold."

"Some fresh air might be nice," Kathleen said.

"Besides, I bid on some of the silent auction items. I have to pick them up at the end of the evening."

"I'm sure they know how to find you and get your money."

"You aren't having such a bad time, are you?"

Kathleen sighed. "You think?"

"It's only twenty minutes till midnight. I promise. We'll leave after that."

Kathleen agreed. She wondered what Joe would do at midnight. It was their first date. Would he kiss her? But then it was New Year's

Eve, everyone kissed at the stroke of midnight. But would it be a long one or just a quick peck on the cheek?

She was too busy with her own kiss at midnight to see what Joe did. Henry had grabbed her with his free arm, the other holding his glass of champagne, and planted a large, wet kiss on her mouth. By the time she looked in Joe's direction, whatever had happened was over. Joe saw her look and shouted, "Happy New Year!"

"It hadn't been such a bad evening, had it?" Henry asked on the drive home.

"No, it was okay."

"Julia seemed nice."

"I guess, if you like that type."

"What type?"

"Ditzy blonde."

"She's hardly a ditzy blonde. She's a well-respected doctor."

"Whatever."

"Are you jealous?"

"Of you and Julia, don't be ridiculous."

"No, of Julia and Joe." Henry turned slightly to catch Kathleen's eyes. Kathleen avoided his gaze, staring at the road ahead of them.

"No. Why should I be?"

"Just checking. Maybe I'm the one who should be jealous," Henry stated.

Kathleen remained silent.

Esther was in the kitchen when Kathleen came inside. "How was the party?" she asked.

"Were you waiting up for me?"

"No, I had just gotten up for a drink of water. I saw the lights from Henry's car and thought I would see how it went."

"It was okay."

"Just okay?"

"You know, I'm really not good at these things. Fancy parties, balls. I'm better off shooting pool and drinking beer."

"I suppose. It sounded like it would have been fun."

"Nah," Kathleen shrugged her shoulders and pulled off her gloves and the cashmere coat, handing the coat to her mom. "Oh, and it seems we may have a new board member for the center. A new doctor in town."

"That's good. Always good to get new members."

"If you say so." Kathleen pulled her hair back down onto her shoulders, freeing it from the tight chignon and yawned. "I'm going to bed," she stated as she went downstairs, escaping the kitchen and her mom's questions. Once again, the thought, "I've got to get out of here," took up residence in her mind.

Chapter 23

They told her it was New Year's Day. Why did it feel like she had already been here for an eternity? How could anyone say suicides are not in heaven? Haven't they already experienced their hell on earth? What could be worse than this? The thoughts floated around in her brain. What else did she have to do but think? Think thoughts that brought no comfort. She needed to shut down her brain. If only she could medicate them away. Instead she tried to sleep them away. When awake, the pressure in her head kept telling her to end it all. So, then she started devising her plan.

Life inside was structured. Everything was taken care of for her, leaving even more time to think thoughts she did not want to acknowledge. There was group in the morning and afternoon. It wasn't mandatory but was encouraged. She didn't want to attend but she started attending faithfully. It was all part of her plan. She wanted "them" to see how she was cooperating in her treatment. She didn't want to give them any excuse to keep her longer.

She figured Walter and Gwen would come to visit. Why bother? One day was like the next in this place. The only reminder of the season was the Christmas tree in the common area. Laura looked at it and memories of Christmases long ago and not so long ago flooded her mind. She remembered the Christmas trees that had decorated her home as a child. Her dad and brothers would go into the woods and cut down a large tree that filled the corner of their front room. Her dad would cut off the lower branches so the tree would fit. Her mom used the branches for decorating the house. The tree dripped sap across the living room floor where her dad dragged it.

"George, why can't you wrap the bottom before dragging that tree through the living room?" her mom would complain every year. Every year it was the same. Her dad just grinned and ignored her as he placed the tree into the stand and tightened the screws. He would look over at Laura and wink.

"How do you like your tree, Laura?" he would ask her.

"I love it, Daddy."

Laura and her mom were left the job of cleaning the sap and needles off the carpet. The smell of evergreen spread throughout the house.

"Mmmm," her mom would stop in the middle of cleaning to breathe in the odor. "Smell it, Laura. Now that's Christmas." After the tree was decorated, they would drink hot chocolate and eat the Christmas sugar cookies her mom had made. Light and fluffy, big cakey cookies with colored sugary sprinkles on some, frosting on others. No one worried about the sugar buzz from cocoa and cookies back then. Her mom had perfected her cocoa. A mixture of cocoa and sugar she blended herself and mixed into hot milk. Mom always used milk in her cocoa. She would have none of those cocoa packets that you mixed with water. It was a little bit of heaven, sitting in front of the newly decorated tree, drinking cocoa and listening to Christmas music. She had wanted to create the same memories for her own children, but Walter had never found the time to cut down a tree, insisting on an artificial tree that could be used every year.

"It's so much easier, Laura. You don't have to worry about watering an artificial tree, or worry about it catching fire, or clean-up needles."

"But it doesn't smell the same."

"If that's a problem, we can spray evergreen scent on the tree. And this way, we can put the tree up at Thanksgiving."

Walter had not understood. It had been easier to let him have his way. But now those memories came back and taunted her. Had she deprived her children of the story book Christmases she remembered? But then had those early Christmases been that story book? She didn't want to remember any more.

Laura met with Dr. Kremer once a week. He was monitoring her meds carefully. After so many years of trying different medications with little result, he wanted to try something different. He also wanted her to undergo a full course of electric shock treatment. She had received them the past summer and shown some improvement.

"I'm wondering if we stopped too soon last time, before getting the full benefit," he told her. The treatment was to start after the New Year. Laura didn't like the treatment, but who was she to argue? She wanted to give the impression of compliance.

"Any questions?" Dr. Kremer asked her.

"When can I get out of here?"

"We'll see. It appears we released you too soon the last time. We want to be extra careful this time to make sure your suicidal ideation is gone."

"So that means? Three weeks? Four weeks?"

"It can take that long for the new medications to start to have an impact. Let's see how it goes. Anything else?"

Joe was pleasantly surprised at the change in Laura the next week. She was up and moving. That was an improvement, he told himself. The sadness was still there, hiding in the back of her eyes. She appeared to be trying to hide it.

Fake it till you make it, Joe remembered the phrase from his work with members of Alcoholic Anonymous. Sometimes if you fake it long enough it can become real to you. Maybe if Laura feigned happiness, eventually it will become real. Not that she was happy in any sense of the word, but she wasn't lying in bed wearing a cloak of depression.

"You seem better this week," Joe commented.

"Can't lie in bed all day. Not if I want to get out of here."

"I hear you are attending the daily group meetings?"

"Yes."

"And ...?" Joe wanted her to continue.

"And I'm attending them. No big deal."

"And electric shock therapy? How is that?" Joe was learning Laura's schedule in order to plan his visits strategically around it. He had tried to visit the day after the treatment, but Laura hadn't been up to having visitors. It had taken a lot out of her.

"Okay. I don't feel anything, and if I did, I don't remember it. It short circuits my memory a bit. That's good."

"Why is that?"

"Some memories are better forgotten."

"Oh, which memories?"

"Forgotten." Laura dismissed his question. "Is that all you came for? To ask me questions?"

"How about you ask the questions."

"How about when can I get out of here?"

"You know I have nothing to do with that."

"But you could put in a good word for me."

"If I have any good words." Joe was surprised by her almost playful attitude. Was it the electric shock therapy? Or something else? What was she hiding? He stared at her before asking, "Do you want to be well?"

"What?"

"Do you want to be well?"

"What are you talking about? What kind of question is that?"

"Jesus healed many people. Some of them he just healed without asking. Some he asked if they wanted to be well. Jesus asked the paralyzed man by the waters of Bethesda if he wanted to be healed. He wouldn't heal someone who didn't want to be healed, couldn't heal someone who didn't want to be healed. Jesus had many questions for his followers. He asked Mary after his resurrection, 'Why do you weep?' and he asked Peter, 'Who do you say that I am?' All good questions. So, I'm asking you, do you want to be well?"

"Of course I want to be well," Laura spit the words out. Finally, some real feelings, Joe thought.

"Okay. I just wanted to know."

The next day Laura stayed in bed rather than go to group. Dr. Kremer noted the change in her behavior.

"It appears that you have stopped attending group." Dr. Kremer looked up from the notes entered by staff. Laura shrugged her shoulders in response. "Did something happen this week? You seemed to be making progress."

Laura slouched in her seat. "Nothing." Dr. Kremer continued to observe her. She shifted a few times before adding, "Pastor Joe asked me if I wanted to be well."

"And ...?"

"Nothing. He said sometimes Jesus made a point of asking a person if they wanted to be well before he would heal them. Seems like a dumb question to me. Who doesn't want to be well?"

"Sounds like a good question to me. Do you want to be well?"

"You too? What a dumb question."

"So, give me an answer." Dr. Kremer continued to watch her. "Do you want to be healed?"

Laura shifted again then, looking down, responded, "No."

"And why not?"

"Because if I was well, I would have to face how I hurt my children with my depression, how I hurt my whole family." Her voice was barely audible. Dr. Kremer waited to allow what Laura had just said to sink in.

"Some problems you just have to go through," he finally said. "There's no avoiding them, no going around them. The only way out is through."

"So, the only way for me to be healed is to deal with my family issues?"

"Yes, that is if you want to be healed. If you are just biding your time, hoping to get out and then finish what you had tried to do before coming here, then no, you don't have to confront these issues. Is that what you are doing?"

Laura didn't answer.

"Sometimes things have to get worse before they can get better."

"How can it get worse?" Laura asked.

"That's for you to answer."

Chapter 24

Kathleen sat down next to her mom at the kitchen table where Esther was drinking her morning coffee. Ever since New Year's Day, she had been looking for an opportunity to talk to her mom alone, something not readily available in this multi-generation household. New Year – a time for new beginnings, a time for resolutions. Kathleen had made a few of her own, but in order to make them happen, she needed her mother's assistance.

"Mom, have you ever thought about taking over the direction of the Center?"

"No. Why should I?"

"I've been thinking. There's nothing to keep me here anymore. Josh and Scott are on their own. You have Peter. Dale has Ava. The Dance Studio and Center for the Arts are on solid ground. There's no reason for me to stick around anymore."

"What are you going to do?"

"I don't know yet. Maybe go back to Chicago. Maybe go to New York."

"And do what?"

"I don't know yet. I was just wondering if you would want to take over as director if I left?"

"Funny you should ask that," Esther started.

"What's funny?" Peter asked. Damn, Kathleen thought, can she never have a private conversation with her mom without Peter or someone else showing up?

"Kathleen was just asking me about running the Arts Center if she left."

"Have you told her our plans yet?" Peter asked. He poured himself a cup of coffee and sat down with them.

"What plans?" Kathleen looked at her mom, ignoring Peter.

"We've booked a condo in Florida for the month of February," Peter answered. "We are going to take our time going down there, visit family on the way. Then maybe we'll drive along the Gulf Coast to Texas before coming back in March."

"And you were going to tell me this when?" Kathleen continued to look at her mom rather than Peter.

"I thought she had already told you." Now both Peter and Kathleen were looking at Esther.

"I was going to tell her," Esther first addressed Peter. "You," she switched to Kathleen. "I was just waiting for the holidays to be over and everything got back to normal. I would have told you soon. I'll make sure everything is taken care of before I leave, and I'll be back in time to take care of taxes in March."

"Or not," Peter interrupted her. Esther put her hand over Peter's hand to keep him from talking.

"Or not, if you think you can handle it. The bookkeeping is not that hard. I'm sure you can do it. But if not, I suppose, maybe Chloe can learn how to do it. Or maybe we can hire someone on a part-time basis."

"Sounds like it's a done deal," Kathleen stated.

"No, dear. It's not."

"Yes, it is," Peter answered at the same time as Esther. "We have the reservations," Peter looked at Esther as he added. "We'll lose our deposit if we don't go."

"We can do that if we have to," Esther said to Peter. She waited to hear what Kathleen had to say.

"No, you can't do that," Kathleen told her. "I won't let you. I can get by. You've given up so much over the years, Mom. It's time you did something for yourself."

"You'll have to take care of Grandpop while I'm gone," Esther said.

"What are you talking about?" Erick walked into the kitchen. "Who has to take care of me?"

"No one, Gramps. Mom and Peter were just telling me about their plans to go to Florida."

"I always enjoyed Florida back when your grandma and I used to go. Of course you should go. I'll keep an eye on Kathleen for you," Erick said.

"You do that, Gramps." Kathleen smiled as she pulled out a chair for her grandfather and brought him a cup of coffee. "We'll be fine together, won't we?"

At eighty-seven, Erick was no longer driving, but still managed to maintain his daily routine. Peter had installed a chair lift to get him up and down the stairs from the main living area to his bedroom. He usually only used it twice a day, coming down in the morning then staying downstairs until ready to go back upstairs and settle in for the night. With assistance he could still maneuver the stairs to get in and out of the house, though Peter and Esther were talking about adding a ramp to make this easier. Maybe in the spring, Peter had said. At his age, he was only one fall away from a wheelchair. Erick was determined to remain as independent as possible, using a cane to get around, his walker packed away in a closet.

"Then it's settled," Peter said. "Florida, here we come."

Chapter 25

The three weeks in Guatemala both dragged and sped by. When she was there, at times she longed to be home in her own comfortable bed, surrounded by her "things." Seeing the poverty around her ... she had been so insulated from this inequity growing up in Cascade Falls. And yet she was still insulated, safe in the protective environment provided by the university. Students were exposed to some of the hardships experienced by the people, and yet protected. Student safety was of utmost importance to the university, so they just touched the tip of what it meant to live in a developing country.

She spent the first week in a language immersion program where she lived with a host family and took Spanish classes during the day. The second week they learned about Latin America in general, Guatemala in specific. They experienced first-hand the poverty of the country. They visited the city dump, the largest in Latin America, where whole families scavenged for items they could sell for meager amounts of cash to buy food. Families lived in shacks alongside the dump. Children ran amidst the trash, helping their parents. Wads of used toilet paper appeared everywhere. The plumbing wasn't able to handle an influx of toilet paper so it ended up in the dump. There was the ever-present danger of sink holes, because the ground was unstable. If not careful, scavengers could be buried alive.

When Gwen had seen videos and pictures of such poverty on TV or social media, it had seemed unreal, made up or blown out of proportion for effect. She had seen the poverty of the slums of India in the movie, Slum Dog Millionaire, but had refused to believe it. Certainly, it was just a story, made up for the movie. People, children, didn't really live like this, did they? And yet here they were. Children not mugging for a camera but real-life children, playing amidst the flies, filth and infestations that were part of the dump. Throwing stones at the rats that shared their playground.

When the sun hit the dump, sparkles from tin foil and metal shone across the pile in a way that was almost beautiful if it weren't so macabre. The children chased after these sparkles. Tin foil could be gathered and sold in the market. There was a beauty in the city dump, but it wasn't those metals. It was in the childish eyes, those that still held out hope, eyes that shown with laughter as they ran and played in the edges of the piles of trash.

Gwen had picked at the food served in the dining area that night. Beans and rice and chicken. Simple fare, yet she couldn't eat it. The few bites she managed to get down threatened to resurface. She picked up her tray and pitched what remained in the trash, feeling guilty for doing so. Better to throw tin foil into the trash for the children to find rather than her beans and rice. She prayed no one would find her thrown-out chicken and attempt to eat it.

Maybe the children would find her leftovers tomorrow or the next day? Her stomach roiled at the thought. Not something she wanted to think about. She managed to keep the few bites she had eaten intact through extreme will.

The third week they visited two different non-profits and participated in a service project at each of them. The university didn't want to leave them without hope. The non-profits were sparkles of hope in a desolate terrain.

The time at the non-profits helped to alleviate the despair that threatened to overcome her after the visits to the dump and other poverty-stricken areas of the country. It helped, but not entirely. It wasn't enough to free her of the images that haunted her brain, filled her sleep. Images of children wearing rags and eating what others had thrown away. What the parents of those children would have done for only a portion of the food that is thrown away each day in the U.S.

She tried to tell herself that there was little that she could do in the face of such poverty, such inequity. The problems were so much bigger than she could begin to wrap her brain around. What little she could do didn't amount to enough to save even one child, much less a whole garbage dump of children. And even if she did manage to save one child, what good would that do for all of the other children?

It would mean something to the one child, her inner voice told her. But how to find that one child? And what would she do when she did? Would she take one child out of a family? What about the family? Surely there must be a way to help? Surely there must be something she could do?

What little she could do would not be enough. She knew that. It was never enough. Not in the face of so much suffering, not in the face of her mother's depression. Gwen had been surprised when her mother's face had popped into her mind, along with all of the children. She thought she had forgotten about her mom. She was taking a vacation from her mom and all of her problems, she told herself.

No, nothing she did was ever enough. Not for her mom. Not for these children. She was not enough. Gwen lay on her cot, staring at the ceiling, allowing her thoughts to flow.

"Gwen, you want to go out?" one of the other students on the trip asked, breaking into her reverie.

"Yeah, Gwen, it's our last night. Come out with us," another member of the group urged. Under other circumstances she would have been happy to go out. She would have loved the opportunity for a night on the town in this new and exciting locale, but she just wasn't up for it.

"Not tonight. I just don't feel like it," Gwen tried to beg off.

"But when will you be in Guatemala again, if ever? Come on," the first student insisted.

"Yeah, you can sit at home in Cascade Falls whenever you want," the second added.

At the mention of Cascade Falls, Gwen was convinced, however reluctantly. They were right. When would she have this opportunity again, she told herself.

The group, accompanied by two faculty members, went to a local restaurant with entertainment. Gwen listened to the music and the laughter around her and started to relax, till she glanced out the window and saw two children begging outside the restaurant. As she watched they were chased away. She was no longer hungry, offering the remains of her meal to her friends.

"Are you okay?" Her instructor's voice broke through the noise around her. "Is something wrong, Gwen?"

"I don't feel very good." The instructor looked over at the other faculty member. He nodded at her.

"I'll go back with you," she told Gwen and led her out of the restaurant.

They walked in silence for a while. Mrs. Peregrine guided her through the darkened streets. They were in a safe part of the city, but that didn't mean they didn't have to be careful. Gwen was grateful for Mrs. Peregrine's presence leading her through the streets, absolving her from the need to pay attention to where she was going.

"I love it here," Mrs. Peregrine finally said.

"Here? How can you? I mean, how can you come back year after year? Seeing the poverty. Doesn't it bother you?"

"I've been bringing students here for the past twelve years. Does it bother me seeing starving children, suffering, and injustice? It does, but I like to believe, have to believe, that what I'm doing is making a difference."

"I used to actually believe in stuff. I don't know now. Does it get any better? After twelve years, has it gotten better?"

"Hard to say. The poverty remains. Jesus himself said the poor you will always have with you. Different non-profits pop up here and there. Some never really make it off the ground. They close within a year. Others though, the ones we visited, they are making a difference. Enough of a difference? It's hard to say. I like to think I'm doing something by bringing students here. That they will be evangelized by the people."

"What? Aren't we supposed to be the ones evangelizing them?"

"Some think that. I don't. I think the poor have a lot to teach us."

"Like what?"

"Like how to appreciate what we have. They also call us to action, to take steps to change the injustices we see. To make the world a better place."

The fresh air and walk helped Gwen. By the time they made it back to the make-shift dorm in a church hall she was no longer woozy and her stomach had settled down.

"You feeling better?" Mrs. Peregrine asked as they entered the building. "Do you want some tea, or a soda?"

"No, I'm okay."

"Let me know if you need anything," she said before leaving.

You can't begin to help me with all I need, Gwen thought but answered, "Sure."

Chapter 26

Kathleen cornered Chloe before dance classes that afternoon. "What do you know about accounting?"

"Nothing. You know that," Chloe answered. "Why?"

"That's what I thought. My mom is going to be gone in February. I need someone to take over for her."

"But didn't you take accounting classes for your business degree?" Both Esther and Kathleen had gone to the local community college and earned associate degrees. Kathleen had gone on to get her bachelor's in business management.

"Yes, but I'm also looking for someone who could do my job. I thought that someone might be you."

"What are you talking about?"

"What would you think about taking over my position? Not right away, but eventually."

"What are you going to do?"

"I don't know yet, but I will. What do you think? I could train you. You could take a few business courses."

"It's not exactly what I dreamed of doing with my life."

"Nor is it what I had planned, but here I am. Think about it." Kathleen spotted Julia coming down the hall. "Crap," slipped out.

"What?" Chloe asked.

Kathleen nodded in Julia's direction. Julia saw her, smiled and headed their way.

"There you are," Julia caught up to Kathleen before she could escape. "I came for my tour. Now show me this amazing dance studio. I'm serious about wanting to be involved in the center." Julia turned to Chloe and extended her hand. "I'm Julia. I'm new to town."

"Chloe," Chloe responded. She raised her eyebrows and looked at Kathleen. "I've got to go, classes are starting. Nice to meet you," she told Julia.

"Totally. Don't let me keep you. I'm here to talk to Kathleen anyway." Julia let go of Chloe's hand. "Now how about that tour you promised me," she told Kathleen. "You remember. At the New Year's Eve party. You promised to show me around."

"Oh, I did? I mean, I did." Kathleen was trying to come up with an excuse.

"Yes, you did." Julia locked arms with Kathleen. "I just know we are going to be friends."

Kathleen looked back at Chloe and caught her laughing as they walked down the hall. Kathleen wasn't sure who was leading whom.

Kathleen didn't understand why Julia was so intent on being friends. Kathleen had no need for friends, and from what she could tell, Julia had no shortage of friends. She appeared to make friends wherever she went. So, what did she want with her?

Kathleen hadn't had a close friend since Joy, but she had friends, she assured herself. She had Chloe and Letty, she told herself, then realized she didn't have any friends outside of the dance studio. She had family, but few friends. Family can be friends, she told herself. Joy had been family and friend. Joe had been a friend, but that had changed when they started dating and now they had broken up. Maybe they could be friends again, but maybe not. Another reason for her to leave.

Julia had requested to be on the Board of Directors of the Center for the Arts. Joe had nominated her and she was readily accepted by the rest of the board.

"You don't mind, do you? That I nominated Julia," Joe had asked Kathleen.

"No, good board members are hard to come by," Kathleen told him.

"That's good, because I don't want it to be awkward."

"You mean because you two are dating?"

"Oh, you know about that." Joe appeared sheepish at the acknowledgment, looking away from Kathleen.

"Well, I did first meet her at the New Year's Eve party. And word gets around fast around here."

"It does. So, it doesn't bother you?" He looked up, hesitantly.

"Not at all. Why should it? Besides, I'm dating someone too. Henry."

"I know. How's that going?"

"Just fine," Kathleen lied. Joe didn't need to know.

Joe and Julia had been dating since New Year's Eve. Julia had no problem with going to Joe's church on Sundays, after attending an earlier service at the Catholic Church. They were seen around town. She was everything Joe could have asked for in a pastor's wife. He didn't know how she did it. Demanding career, single mom, and yet she made time for him. Her daughter, Alexandria, was the same age as Stephanie, his oldest. Alex was away at school, but knew about her mother's new relationship, having been instrumental in setting up their first date.

Julia had told him about Alex's father. A U.S. Marine, he had died while serving in the Middle East, leaving her to raise Alex on her own. Joe could certainly appreciate how hard that could be.

"And yet you managed med school while raising your daughter." he had commented when Julia shared the story.

"Well, I didn't do it alone. Does anyone raise children entirely alone? I don't know how they do it. My parents were awesome. I don't know what I would have done without them to watch Alex while I went to school." And she had a healthy relationship with her parents, both parents. Was there anything that wasn't perfect about this woman, Joe asked himself.

And she wanted to be involved in the community. Besides the work at the clinic on Wednesday, she wanted to be involved in the Center for the Arts. What didn't she do?

Chapter 27

Laura stared out the window in the common area to the sidewalks and streets below. Snow was flying by, lightly adding to the layer already on the ground, covering the dirt that had accumulated over the past few days. Christmas decorations were gone. Laura was glad. No artificial lights glaring at her, daring her to be jolly. Ho, ho, ho, no more. She preferred the snow-covered expanse. People walked, some rushing to their destination, others carefully maneuvering the slippery sidewalks, others slipping. Children slid on their way to school on the sidewalk across the street from the hospital. How could they be so normal? Had they no idea who was observing them from above? Real nut cases. Laura didn't count herself as one of them.

Trapped. She was trapped in this building, trapped in this body, trapped in this life. There was nothing that gave her a reason to go on. No points of light in her dark life. What did she have to look forward to? What reason to continue? Her own children were gone and not interested in her. How long had it been since they had been like those children, slipping off to school, sliding away from her? She hadn't been able to hold on to them anymore than she was able to hold those children below. She longed to break out, grab those children and hug them close. But then everyone would know the truth. She was a nut case, genuine, certified.

And soon her one remaining child would be gone. What would she do to hold her close? What would work? It's too late. Too late for so many of her dreams. They were buried under snow. Her only recourse had been taken from her, at least for now. They wouldn't let her out if they thought she was still plotting her own demise. And why not? They — her doctor, the psych nurses, the pastor, not even her husband — couldn't give her a reason to keep on with this useless vapor some called life.

What had she dreamed of once? It had been so long, she couldn't remember. What had she dreamed as a long-legged school girl sliding her way through school? The effort to think hurt.

"Laura, are you going to join group?" a staff member called to her. Laura walked over and sat down in an empty chair. Might as well get this over with.

"The last time we met, I asked you, did you want to be made well?" Joe tried to pick up where they had left off.

"Yeah, so?" Laura responded.

"Just wondering if you had thought about it."

"Why should I? I told you then, of course I want to be well."

"Just checking."

"But if I didn't want to be well, what is it to you?"

"I guess the better question is, what is it to you?"

Laura frowned. Joe could tell she did not like this line of questioning, didn't like it when he turned questions back on her.

"You aren't my therapist. You are my pastor. You are supposed to provide answers, not more questions."

"That what you think?"

"It isn't what I think. It just is."

"I don't know, seems to me Jesus had a lot of questions for his followers. He had more questions than answers at times. And his answers were often framed as a story or parable."

"So, tell me a story, Pastor."

"Okay. How about the story of the woman bent over for fourteen years, who refused to be healed?"

"Never heard of it. I don't think that's from the Bible."

"That's because it's not. We primarily hear about Jesus' successful healings. Maybe his followers didn't want to bother with any unsuccessful attempts, but we do hear about the rich young man that Jesus invited to follow him. The rich young man wasn't willing to give up his possessions so he walked away. Jesus was sad about this. I imagine there were other situations where Jesus wasn't able to heal a person because they didn't want to be healed. Jesus wasn't going to force anyone."

"I find that hard to believe."

"Believe what you will. Even Jesus can't heal someone who doesn't want to be healed. It would go against their free will. God didn't give us free will to use only if we do what God wants us to do. God won't violate his gift to us."

"Are you saying I don't want to be healed?"

"I'm not saying that. Are you?"

"I just want everyone to leave me alone, let me out of here."

"And what will you do?" Laura refused to answer. Joe continued, "Have you thought about how this is affecting your family?"

"I haven't thought of anything else. Don't I know what a terrible wife and mother I've been? I don't need to be reminded of it." Laura's face flushed with anger as she dared him to continue with his questions.

"And you think trying to kill yourself will solve that problem?" Joe continued, undeterred by her response.

"At least I won't be a burden any more to anyone, especially Gwen."

Joe paused at the mention of Gwen. Was this the key to reaching her? "And what do you think Gwen would say about that?"

"I think she would be relieved to be free of me."

"Have you asked her?"

"Don't you think I know that she can't wait to get out of here and never look back, just like her brothers and sister. I'd be doing her a favor." Laura's anger melted into sadness as she looked away.

"I don't believe Gwen would see it that way, but let's say she did. What about you? What if Gwen were gone? What would you do then?"

"What do you mean?" Laura cautiously looked at him.

"Aside from your children and your family, what would give meaning to your life? What do you want to do just for you?"

"I don't think I want anything." Laura looked away again.

"There must be something you want for yourself. Think about it. When you were a child, or when you were Gwen's age, what did you want for yourself?"

"When I was Gwen's age, I was already married and pregnant. I dropped out of school to help put Walter through med school and raise the baby."

"Then before that. Wasn't there something you wanted?" Joe continued to push despite her resistance to his questions.

"I don't know. That's so long ago."

"When you stand in the spot that is just you and your God, when you face God, what is it that you want?"

"I just don't want to hurt anymore." Laura turned away and looked at the floor as this admission slipped out of her mouth. Joe leaned forward. He thought about taking her hand then decided against it. He figured if he pushed too much, she would close back up. "Will the pain ever end?" Laura asked.

Finally, something to work with, Joe thought. "And if you had that pain-free life, what would you do with it?"

"I wish I could make it up to my children for all of the times I wasn't there for them, but especially Gwen. I did okay with her brothers and sister. It's Gwen who suffered the most. She's been a mother to me. Daughters are not supposed to take care of their mothers. It's supposed to be the other way around. Mothers take care of their daughters." Joe saw tears well up in the corners of her eyes as Laura resisted.

"And what if you can't make it up to her? You can't change the past."

"Then I might as well be dead." A light went out, as Laura closed the door to further questioning along those lines.

"We are going in circles, aren't we? Would you do something for me?" Laura nodded her head slightly, just enough to acknowledge his question. "I want you to think about that place inside, that place where it is just you and your God. Can you do that?"

"I don't know."

"Try. Think about that place, imagine you are with Jesus. Ask him, 'what would you have me do?' Can you do that for me?"

"I guess. I'll try. What would it hurt?" Laura agreed.

"Close your eyes and imagine that Jesus is sitting right here with you. What is he saying?" Joe sat quietly with Laura, praying that, just maybe, Laura was entering into the experience rather than resisting. After a few minutes he asked, "Do you need more time?"

Laura took a deep breath before answering, "No."

"What happened?" Joe asked carefully, quietly. He didn't want to interrupt the peace that had spread across her face. "What did Jesus say?"

"One word. He said 'rest.'" A tear slid down her cheek.

"Rest?" Joe wondered about this. Wasn't that part of the problem? She had been sleeping too much? But looking at Laura's face, he realized she had heard what she was meant to hear. "And, what are you going to do?"

"I think that just maybe I'll be able to sleep tonight, a restful sleep. That would be lovely." She wiped away the tear.

"Then you do that. We'll talk more next week."

Chapter 28

The house was strangely silent once her mom and Peter were gone. First Josh and Scott had left, taking with them their youthful energy. Now her mom and Peter were gone. Not that they had been noisy. Still their presence had been felt. Now that presence was no longer here.

"So, Gramps, it's just you and me now," Kathleen said to her grandfather after watching her mom and Peter pull out of the driveway.

"Just so I don't have to eat your cooking."

"Come on. It's not that bad."

"I can still fry an egg. I'll make breakfast," Erick told her as he walked past her to the kitchen.

"Deal," Kathleen said. It might not be so bad, she told herself. Gramps was no trouble, and he could cook some.

"What's happening with you and that lawyer?" Erick asked over breakfast.

"Henry? Not much."

"You still dating?"

"Sure." Kathleen had found herself pulling away from Henry after New Year's Eve. It wasn't that she didn't like him, she just didn't like him enough. He was okay but he wasn't enough to keep her from leaving Cascade Falls. That was what she wanted. She didn't want any involvement that might keep her from leaving. She didn't have any plan in mind but was working on it. A serious relationship would interfere with those plans.

"He seemed nice. If you want to invite him over, I'll cook."

"That's okay, Gramps. You don't have to try to take Mom's place."

"Didn't say I was. Just making an offer."

"I appreciate it. I'll let you know if I want to take you up on it. So, what's on your agenda for the day?"

"Got a full day. I'm taking the bus to the senior center for lunch and bingo. What about you?"

"The usual. Going to work. I won't be home till after seven. You okay with that?"

"Why wouldn't I be?"

"It's just usually someone is around here at night."

"You don't have to babysit me," Erick insisted.

"Wouldn't think of it."

"Now you get ready for work and I'll do the dishes."

"Whatever you say."

Kathleen was discovering that it wasn't bad, sharing the house with her grandfather. He gave her an easy excuse to beg out of dates.

"I have to get home to Grandpop," she would tell Henry when he asked.

"I could come over, could bring dinner for all three of us," he offered.

"Not today, but I'll keep that in mind."

"Did I do something wrong?" Henry asked.

"No, not at all."

"It's just that you've been different since New Year's Eve. Are you mad at me?"

"Believe me, if I were mad at you, you would know."

"And if something was wrong, you would tell me?"

"Of course," again Kathleen lied. This was becoming quite a habit, lying to the men in her life.

"Then why don't I believe you?" Henry commented.

"Okay, dinner, Saturday night. You bring it over." Kathleen finally agreed.

Chapter 29

Two weeks after getting home from Guatemala and it all seemed like it had never happened. Gwen tried to push it out of her mind as she headed into her last semester of school. She had other things to keep her busy, fill up her mind, such as what she would do when she graduated, and her senior project. Still thoughts of Guatemala invaded her space. What struck Gwen most was how happy the people were. They had so little, yet what they had they shared. And they were happy. Lacking all of the material comforts of her home, they were so much happier than she was. Was it the sunshine and warm weather? Lack of sun does contribute to depression. Why were they so happy when there was so much depression in the United States where we had so much? Was there a connection?

And then there was her mom. Gwen had expected her to be home by now. This was the longest her mom had been hospitalized, over six weeks. Gwen had not been in a hurry to see her mom after she got back. She was afraid of what she would see. When she last visited her before going to Guatemala, her mom had seemed okay. She had talked about getting out. Her mom had been determined to do whatever it took to be able to get out. That was another reason why Gwen was surprised when her mom had not made it home yet. Had her mom been faking it when she talked about getting better? It wouldn't have been the first time, Gwen knew that. In the past her mom would say anything, do anything, to get out and stay out of the hospital. She did not like it there, but then, she didn't like it anywhere as far as Gwen could tell.

Gwen didn't know what the hurry was for her mom to get home when her mom was far from happy here. But her mom could put on a good show. Perhaps that was where Gwen had gotten her ability to act. In high school she had run to get away from her problems. Now she acted. If she acted happy long enough, would she eventually be happy? Gwen liked losing herself in her character. It was better than the act she put on for the world. The only person who got her was Marcie, and Marcie was gone.

"Hi Mom," Gwen sat down at a table across from her mom. She hated visiting her mom in the hospital, hated the antiseptic smells, hated seeing her mom in hospital garb. Of course, many days at home her mother never got out of her pajamas, draping her bathrobe around her body as she slouched through the house. But that was a step up from the hospital gown.

"Gwen, I've missed you," her mom said. Gwen didn't respond. "How was your trip to Guatemala? Tell me all about it."

Like you would be interested, Gwen wanted to spit out. Instead she said, "It was okay. Hard. A lot of poverty. How are you?"

"Oh, about the same. You know how it is in here. Not much happening."

"No, I don't know how it is in here, and I hope I never do," Gwen surprised herself when she said this.

"Now, Gwen," her dad stopped her.

"No, it's okay. Let her say what she has to say. I hope you never do either," her mom stopped her dad.

"I'm sorry, Mom. That didn't come out right."

"No, it's all right. I need you to be honest with me. Can you do that?"

"Sure, Mom," Gwen lied.

"If I'm ever to get better, I can't have people tip-toing around my feelings like I'm a porcelain princess."

"Whatever you say, Mom." Gwen wasn't sure about this new mom. This wasn't what she was used to. She didn't know whether she liked her or not.

Chapter 30

Laura held onto that word, "rest." Before, she had been sleeping a lot, but it wasn't a restful sleep. It had been a disrupted, drug-induced sleep that left her feeling tired and in need of sleep all day. She had begged for more drugs to help her sleep. Even then she would toss and turn, never getting a full night's sleep. She had spent her days dozing and exhausted from her lack of a peaceful sleep. She had begged for a stronger dose to help her sleep in the past, but now she requested that she no longer be given any drugs at night. Dr. Kremer attributed this to the electric shock therapy kicking in. Laura didn't bother to tell him otherwise. She was just pleased to be able to sleep and not wake up in a drug-induced haze.

"You are making progress," Dr. Kremer said at their next meeting. "Perhaps we have finally got the right meds and the right balance. You've been doing well in group and in your individual sessions. I'm going to have you try a different form of therapy, DBT – Dialectical Behavior Therapy. There is a therapist in town trained in this. I'm going to see about her meeting with you here first. Then you can continue seeing her when you get out of here."

"When I get out of here? When will that be?"

"If you continue to make progress, it could be as soon as next week." Laura's heart pounded and her stomach sunk at the same time.

"This is the first you've said anything about me getting out," Laura said. Before it had been her asking, him refusing to give her a time frame.

"How do you feel about that?"

"Excited, I guess. Scared, too."

"That's normal. It can be hard to adjust to being back in your home environment. We can discuss it further next week."

Laura was unsure about leaving. She was sleeping better. It seemed the black fog that had engulfed her for years had lifted. But she was afraid. What if it came back? What would she do then? How did she know it wouldn't come back?

Laura wasn't comfortable with Dr. Janet Holton at first. Was this going to be another therapist probing her deep, dark, inner secrets from childhood? She had been through that before, had had enough of it.

"Are you going to ask me about my past?" Laura asked Dr. Holton.

"Only if you want me to," Dr. Janet smiled. Laura felt herself relax. "What I'm going to do is teach you new ways to process information in the present rather than dwelling in the past." Dr. Janet looked through Laura's case file.

"I see you've attempted suicide several times."

Laura shook her head yes. She wasn't sure how else to respond. She couldn't lie about it when it was all there in the paperwork, in black and white.

"And so, how did that work for you?"

"Not very good, obviously. I'm still here."

"Or maybe you're still here because you want to be here."

"Oh, no, that wasn't the case." Laura shifted in her seat. Yet another therapist trying to tell her what she wanted.

"Think about it though. You're a Christian, aren't you?"

"Yes. Minimal." Laura shrugged her shoulders.

"And what does your church say about suicide?"

"It's frowned upon."

"And why do you want to die?"

"Because I want to escape all my pain."

"What guarantee do you have of that? How do you know that will end your pain? Maybe you will continue to suffer after death?"

"I guess some would call that hell."

"I can't say what will happen after you die, but I can guarantee this." Dr. Janet took Laura's hands and looked intently into her eyes. "I guarantee that if you stick with me and work this process, you will have better days. You've had better days in the past, and there will be better days in the future. But if you kill yourself that will not happen." Dr. Janet paused before adding, "I also promise that it won't be easy. You will have bad days, but I will be with you through those days. I'll help you, if you are willing to work with me."

Laura wasn't sure what to say. Janet's dark blue eyes were probing her own. She couldn't bear the warmth in those eyes.

"You don't have to decide today. Think about it and we'll talk again next week."

Laura didn't need to think further. She looked up. "I'll give it a try. I do want better days."

"And you will have them," Dr. Janet assured her.

Chapter 31

"You know, your mom is in a fragile condition." It was one of the few nights that she and her dad were home together for dinner. Most nights he worked late. Gwen left for rehearsal or classes before her dad got home. "Having your support would mean a lot to her."

"When has Mom not been fragile?" Gwen asked. "When have I not been supportive?"

"I didn't mean it that way." Gwen watched her dad struggle to find the right words.

"Forget it, Dad. I have to go," Gwen got up, cleared her plate and prepared to leave. She had had enough of her mom's problems. The Bible said we are our brother's keeper, nothing about being our mother's keeper. Her dad followed her into the kitchen.

"I'll take care of these," her dad told her, putting his dishes in the sink with hers. "They are talking about your mother coming home in a week or so. She will need you. She'll need both of us."

"Sure, Dad. Whatever." When had she not taken care of her mother? Was she ever to be free of this burden, or would she be trapped forever with this selfish woman who was her mother? Gwen held back her words and excused herself. "I have to get to play practice."

"When is your play again? Maybe your mom will be well enough to attend."

"Sure, Dad," Gwen restated. "It's in three weeks. Two weekends in a row. I'll text you the dates. Now I've got to go." Gwen didn't understand the anger trying to break through. She had never been one to be angry, had always been upbeat, even amidst all the trials at home. It had been part of her carefully made mask. She was the fun one, the life of the party. She couldn't get angry. So, she pushed it down into her calf and toes and ran it off when she had time. Most of the time she denied any anger. But there was something about what she had seen and experienced in Guatemala that had awakened her sleeping anger. She told herself she was angry about what she had seen, but there was more to it. Others in her travel cohort had been angry as well, but not as angry as Gwen. The surface anger from the three-week trip had ripped open the carefully assembled box where she had neatly collected her anger over the years.

There was no duct tape of the soul to repair the breach, no holding it back. It came out in streams of depression she refused to acknowledge. If she kept busy, she could beat this, she told herself. How could she be depressed when she was so active, so busy? She knew depression from her mother. Her mother, wrapped in her gown of depression, was unable to do anything. This was not depression. She could push through it. She was not her mother!

Chapter 32

Joe noticed something was up with his secretary. Her work wasn't falling behind. She continued to excel, was going above and beyond what he expected of her. No, it was something else. She was a mass of energy, just waiting to explode. He knew about her class load as well as the time being put into rehearsals. He also knew something about the cross-cultural trip, though Gwen had chosen not to tell him much about it, insisting she had too much work to do to take time to tell him. And, of course, there was the situation with her mother. Yes, she had plenty of reason to be ready to explode.

He didn't know exactly what was going on. He just knew that he was afraid she would burst all of a sudden, come crashing down, and he would be left without a secretary once again. Why did he keep hiring these young women? He needed someone more stable.

Joe was afraid that any comment that was less than positive would send Gwen spiraling out of control. And then what would he do? Edna was safely tucked away in Florida where he could not reach her. How would he manage? There was always the school secretary. She had helped out at times. But then Gwen was a church member. He was concerned about her well-being. Here he was, heading into the busiest months of the church year. It would be hard to get through them without a secretary he could rely on.

He didn't discuss any of this with Julia. He didn't want their times together to be filled with his work, or her work. They were just getting to know each other. He wanted the relationship to unfold slowly, carefully. However, Julia was careening on her own path of overwork and over extension. Besides her already busy work schedule, time at the clinic, and now being on the board of Joy's Center for the Arts, she was taking on fundraising for the Center. He was caught between too overly busy, stressed-out women – one at work, one during his leisure time. He wondered which one would explode first? When he tried suggesting that Julia slow down a little, he was shot down.

"I appreciate your commitment to the Center, but don't you think you are stretching yourself too thin," he had suggested.

"Oh, no. I've been busier than this before. This is nothing."

He wondered what was pushing her to this extreme. What was she trying to prove? She had already achieved so much more than so many women her age. Why couldn't she rest on her laurels?

"Besides," Julia continued, "this is your busy time, isn't it? Lent and then Easter. You'll be too busy to notice if I'm not around."

"That isn't exactly the point," he tried to explain.

"Don't worry, honey. I'll always have time for you," she said and kissed him. "Oh, and I've volunteered to head up the May fundraiser dinner. It'll be amazing."

Chapter 33

Could this day get any worse? Kathleen wondered as she drove home. Now not only does she have to deal with Julia on her board, Henry was on it too.

"You need a lawyer on your board," he had insisted, essentially self-nominating himself for the position. The rest of the board had been delighted at the addition. They were still dating but she wasn't sure how comfortable she was with having him on her board too. Just a little too close for comfort. She wasn't ready for that yet.

And if that wasn't enough, now Julia had taken over their May fundraiser.

"Don't worry about anything. I've done this before. You shouldn't have to deal with all of this fundraising. I'll take care of everything. All you'll have to do is show up. I'll make it a premiere fundraising event, much like the hospital gala. In fact, I'll see if I can get the same venue. We'll attract more people with money with a better location. It will be epic," Julia had said at the meeting.

"What about people who can't afford the high price that such a space requires? I don't want this to become an event only for the rich and powerful in our community," Kathleen inserted her complaint. No one heard. They were all caught up in Julia's gossamer web. How did she get people to like her so easily?

Kathleen felt her control of the Center for Arts slipping away from her. Much as she wanted an active board and to get the Center on a solid financial basis in order to be able to leave, now that it appeared to be happening, she wasn't sure she liked it. She was not ready to give up control.

She pulled into the driveway and noted that several lights were on downstairs. Grandpop couldn't still be up, could he? Must have left the lights on when he went upstairs for the night, Kathleen thought as she pulled into the garage.

She walked into the kitchen and found her grandfather on the floor.

"Gramps, are you okay?" she rushed to his side and touched him to make sure he was awake.

"No, I just decided to take a nap on the floor." Kathleen gave a sigh of relief. He still had his humor. Couldn't be too bad.

"What happened?"

"I fell. Couldn't get back up. Seems this leg just won't work."

"Where is your call button?"

"Upstairs on my nightstand."

"That's a good place for it. Does your leg hurt?"

"It did at first but it's not so bad as long as I don't move. Help me get up."

Kathleen put her arm around his back and started to lift, only to hear him cry out in pain. "You aren't going anywhere," she said, lowering him back down. "I'm calling an ambulance."

When Erick didn't complain at the suggestion, Kathleen was worried. She called 911 then tried to make her grandfather more comfortable on the floor, covering him with a blanket and tucking a pillow under his head.

When the ambulance arrived, the EMTs lifted him onto a gurney and wheeled him out.

"It looks like he may have broken his hip," the first EMT said. "Do you want to ride in the ambulance or come in your own car?"

Kathleen stood aside feeling helpless as they wheeled her grandfather out. He looked so fragile lying on that board. She grabbed her purse and locked the door behind her.

"Yes, with you," she said, climbing into the ambulance after him. She would worry about how to get home later.

They rode through town at regular speed, lights flashing but no siren. Not an emergency, Kathleen assured herself. Maybe she should have driven herself she thought, then held her grandfather's hand. No, she needed to be here. Who should she call, she wondered. Not her mom and Peter. She didn't want to interrupt their vacation. Besides, what could they do from Florida? Not Josh or Scott. They would want to know but she didn't want them skipping classes, at least not until she knew how serious it was. She remembered following behind the ambulance three years ago when her grandfather had had a heart attack. Joe had come then. She wasn't going to call him for this. She hated to call her brother Dale. He was probably getting ready for bed, if not already in bed. But no, he would want to know. Kathleen called him from the Emergency Room while waiting for the ER staff to get her grandfather settled into a room.

"Do you want me to come?" Dale asked.

"No, no need for that. I'll let you know what happens. No sense in both of us losing sleep." Kathleen flashed back to that other night in the ER three years ago. She had stayed with her grandfather all night, sleeping in his room in the cardiac care unit. She was relieved when she was allowed back into the ER and saw him partially sitting up in bed.

"I'm sorry you have to go through this," Erick told her.

"What are you talking about old man? You sure know how to show a girl a good time. What else do I have to do? I could use a night out."

"Not like this."

"You let me determine what I would rather do. Sit home in an empty house or spend the night with these cute medical students and interns."

It was several hours before Erick got a room upstairs in the main hospital.

"It appears he has a broken hip. We'll have an orthopedic surgeon talk to you tomorrow about your options," the ER doctor told them. "In the mean time we'll admit you, get you to a better room," he told Erick.

Kathleen waited until her grandfather was settled into his room and was sleeping before leaving. One o'clock. Too late to call anybody to come get her. She called for a cab. She slept fitfully through the night, flipping from one side to the other in an attempt to sleep. She was up early and back at the hospital by seven. Dale joined her on his way to work. He arrived just as his grandfather was being wheeled out for more x-rays.

"Did you stay all night?" he asked her.

"No, but I might have for all the sleep I got."

"You look terrible."

"Thanks."

"No, I mean did you get any sleep?"

"Not much."

"Let me get you something to eat," Dale insisted. Kathleen hesitated. "Come on, it'll be at least an hour before Grandpop gets back." They went down to the hospital cafeteria.

"Have you called Mom yet?" Dale asked over breakfast.

"No, I'm waiting till I know something more."

"Yeah, no sense in getting her worried."

"Oh, she'll be worried, no matter what. I'd just rather have answers to the many questions she'll have before I call her."

Dale looked about the cafeteria, tapping his foot as he sipped his coffee.

"He'll be okay," Kathleen put her hand on his shoulder. He stopped bouncing his foot momentarily but started again as soon as she removed her hand.

"It's been a while since we've been here," he commented.

"Yes, it's been nice, not coming here." There had been a period a few years ago when it had seemed like they were always at the hospital. First for Joy, then for other incidents. Kathleen hadn't missed the place. She was surprised by a familiar voice.

"Dale, Kathleen, what brings you here? The kids okay?"

"Pastor," Dale jumped up to shake Joe's hand. "Good to see you. The kids are fine. It's our grandfather."

"He fell last night, while I was at the board meeting," Kathleen remained seated.

"Why didn't you call me?" Joe asked.

"It wasn't an emergency. I didn't want to bother you," Kathleen answered.

"Hi, Kathleen," another familiar voice was heard. "What's this about your grandfather?" Julia. Wasn't it bad enough she had to deal with her at board meetings?

"We think he broke his hip," Dale answered for Kathleen.

"I'm sorry. Is there anything I can do?" Julia asked.

"Not unless you're an orthopedic surgeon," Kathleen responded.

"No, I guess I can't help there. Let me know if something comes up. I've got to go." She turned to Joe and kissed him. "Oh, awesome meeting last night," she told Kathleen as she left.

"I better go too," Joe said. "I've got some people to visit. I'll stop and see your grandfather later. What is his room number?"

Dale wrote down the number. "Thank you, Pastor. That would be great." Dale shook Joe's hand again before he left.

"Well, that was rude," Dale told Kathleen when he sat back down.

"Why? Just because I don't jump up at the pastor's approach."

"You hardly acknowledged Julia. What do you have against her?"

"She's just too ... too... Do I have to have a reason?"

"I guess not. It doesn't have anything to do with the fact that she's dating Pastor Joe, does it?"

"Of course not. He's nothing to me. He's ... too nice."

"If you say so."

They finished up their breakfast and returned to their grandfather's room just as he was being wheeled back in.

"Can't a guy get something to eat around here?" Erick asked before the transport team left. His nurse came in after them.

"Sorry, Mr. Gaines. Doctor's orders. No food in case they want to do surgery today."

"And when will I know that?" Erick asked.

"As soon as the orthopedic surgeon has a chance to look at your x-rays and go over your chart," she told him.

"Do you think he will be in this morning?" Dale asked. "I'm just wondering whether I should wait or go to work."

"Dr. Evans usually does his rounds around eleven. Sometimes earlier, sometimes later, especially if he is in surgery in the morning."

"You don't have to stay here on my account," Erick said.

"Yes, I do. There's no talking me out of it," Dale told him.

"Thanks, Dale," Kathleen said. "I'd like to have another person to discuss options with."

"What's there to discuss? If it's broke, fix it. If it's not, get me out of here," Erick said.

"It could be more complicated than that," Dale told him. He had learned that from his years caring for Joy.

"Just so I get something to eat," Erick grumbled.

Joe stopped by Erick's room around eleven, after finishing his other visits. Dale was working on his laptop while Erick watched TV and Kathleen napped in a chair. She jumped up when she heard his voice.

"Oh, I thought you were the doctor," she said.

"Good to see you, too," Joe responded.

"We're expecting the surgeon any time now to tell us the results of the x-rays," Dale explained.

"So, you don't know anything yet?" Joe asked.

"Just what they told us last night," Kathleen said.

"And how are you doing through all of this?" Joe moved over to the bed to talk to Erick.

"I'd be doing better if these kids here would just let me be," Erick said.

"Well, you know how kids can be. They have minds of their own," Joe said.

"Especially that one," Erick pointed at Kathleen with pride. "No one can tell her what to do."

"Amen," Joe said in agreement, looking over at Kathleen and laughing.

"I'm glad you find me so entertaining. At least I'm good for that," Kathleen said as she continued to wake up, wiping her eyes with the back of her hands.

Dr. Evans came in followed by the attending nurse and a med student. The nurse was filling him in on details from Erick's charts as he looked it over. He handed the chart to the student then introduced himself. After introductions he pulled up a chair next to Erick's bed and spoke directly to him.

"How are you today?" he asked.

"I'd be a lot better if I could have something to eat."

"Well, we'll talk about that. You've got a pretty good break there," he said to Erick and to the gathered family. "The top of the ball joint on the femur has cracked. They call it a broken hip, but actually it's the femur." Dr. Evans indicated where the break was located by pointing to his own leg.

"Does that mean surgery?" Erick asked.

"Well, that depends. At your age, we don't always recommend surgery. Sometimes we'll let it go if the patient isn't in pain and the bone is still aligned. Only you will probably be confined to a wheel chair for the rest of your life."

"And if we opt for surgery?" Kathleen asked.

"There's still a chance that he won't be able to walk again, but there is more hope that he would be able to walk if he has the surgery. He is in reasonably good health for his age. It's entirely up to you."

"So, in the one scenario, I'm confined to a wheel chair and in the other scenario I undergo surgery and the pain associated with that and I may still end up in a wheel chair," Erick said.

"Or with physical therapy you may be able to walk," Dr. Evans said.

"I don't like those options. How about a third option? Just take me out to the back forty and shoot me."

"Grandpop!" Kathleen and Dale said together.

"Look, I've lived a good life. Why do I need to prolong it? I'm good with God. I'm ready to join my wife. We've been too many years apart."

"That's not an option," Joe intervened.

"Well, it should be," Erick insisted.

"I see you need some time to talk this over," Dr. Evans stood up.

"Wait, Doc," Erick said. "If I want the surgery what then?"

"We'll schedule you for tomorrow morning, so no solid food until after the surgery. You'll spend some time here recuperating then you'll be sent to a rehab facility."

"I don't have the option of rehab at home?"

"Do you have someone to take care of you?"

"Me," Kathleen stepped forward. "He has me."

"Maybe after a couple of weeks. It depends on how rehab goes," Dr. Evans said.

"And if I don't have the surgery?"

"We'll get you something to eat, monitor how you are doing and either send you to a long-term care facility in a wheel chair, or home in a wheel chair, if you have sufficient care available."

"I think I'd rather take my chances with the surgery," Erick said.

"If that's what you want," Dr. Evans told him.

"It's not what I want. What I want is to get up and walk out of here. But we don't always get what we want, do we?"

"No, we don't," Dr. Evans looked about the room. "Any questions?"

"Yes, doctor," Kathleen said. "Did he break the bone when he fell, or did he fall because the bone was broken?"

"At his age, it's hard to say. His bones are pretty porous. There's a good chance it was already broken before he fell."

"So, even if he hadn't fallen, the bone was already broken?" Kathleen said.

"Quite possibly. No fall is good at his age, but we can't prevent every fall, or every broken bone. If it hadn't happened last night, it was most likely just a matter of time," Dr. Evans said.

"Thank you. I just wanted to know," Kathleen said.

"What does it matter?" Dale asked.

"It matters because in the one case, maybe if I had been home, I could have prevented the fall, prevented all of this."

Joe shook his head. "You aren't to blame," He quietly assured her.

"Anyone else?" Dr. Evans looked around the room. "Okay. We'll schedule your surgery for tomorrow. Your nurse will tell you later today once the surgery schedule is set." Dr. Evans shook hands with everyone before heading out with his intern.

"Not what you wanted to hear," Joe commented. With the departure of the doctor, it felt like all the air had left the room. They were left in a vacuum where it was hard to breathe.

"I guess I better call Mom. She'll want to know. And Josh and Scott," Kathleen said but made no movement towards her phone.

"And I guess I better get to work so I can be here tomorrow," Dale said but remained in the room.

"Stop the long faces," Erick was the only one with any energy remaining. "I'm not dead yet. And if I die on the table, then I'll have my third option."

"Don't talk like that, Grandpop. You aren't going to die on the table," Kathleen insisted.

"Then I'll have no more sad faces. And if you can't manage that, then get out of here."

"Sorry, Gramps, but I'm not leaving, so I guess you'll have to put up with me the way I am," Kathleen said.

"Stubborn child," Erick shook his head. "See what I told you," he said to Joe.

"Don't I know." Joe said a short prayer with the family then assured them he would be back tomorrow. Dale and Kathleen walked out with him, Dale to get to work, Kathleen to find a quiet place to make her phone calls.

"He's one tough guy," Joe assured them as they walked down the hall. "If anyone will make it, your grandfather will."

"Yes, but what kind of a life will it be for him, stuck in a wheel chair. If the surgery doesn't kill him, being confined to a wheel chair will," Kathleen said.

"Well, we'll deal with that when we have to. For now, we just have to get him through this surgery," Dale told her.

Kathleen found an empty waiting room to make her calls while Dale and Joe left.

Esther wanted to leave immediately when getting the news.

"Mom, what can you do? Even if you drive all night you won't get here before his surgery and what would you do once you got here?" Kathleen could almost see her mom's face as she spoke. She knew her mom was not listening but kept talking anyway hoping to get through to her. "He's not going to be in any shape for visitors for a while. He'll be in the hospital, then maybe a rehab facility before coming home. There's nothing you can do here. You might as well enjoy your vacation."

"How can I enjoy my vacation when I'm worried about my dad?"

"Okay. Then worry down there where there's sunshine and try to get some rest. Don't worry. There will be plenty for you to do once you get back and Grandpop's out of the hospital," Kathleen and Peter finally convinced her.

"I suppose … You'll call us as soon as you know anything."

"Of course, Mom. Don't worry. I'll call."

Josh and Scott were also worried but were more easily talked into waiting.

"See how it goes. No sense in skipping classes or work. Maybe you can visit on the weekend," she suggested.

The surgery took longer than expected. The bone was in worse shape than the surgeon anticipated. He removed more bone before being able to attach the rod to the remaining bone. Still, Erick did well during the surgery and the doctor anticipated a full recovery. Now it was up to Erick and time.

The house was strangely quiet when Kathleen came home each night after being at the hospital. She wondered, how could she have complained about it being a geriatric ward? How could she have wanted to leave? Now she just wanted someone, another voice, to fill the void that was the house she called home for so many years. It wasn't home. Not without her mom and grandfather. But it would be home again. Her grandfather would be home soon, she told herself.

Chapter 34

Now that the day had arrived, Laura was unsure about going home. What would she find? What kind of welcome from her daughter? Gwen only came to see her a few times, by mutual consent, she figured. Laura realized how busy Gwen was.

"You mustn't think you have to stay home to babysit me," Laura told Gwen before coming home. "Understand?"

"Sure, Mom," Gwen said but Laura could tell she didn't believe it. Did she blame Gwen? Not at all. She wouldn't have believed her either. How could Gwen believe that it was going to be different this time? Laura wasn't sure she believed it herself, but she was going to try her best. That was more than she could have said the last time.

Pastor Joe was going to continue visiting her and she set up weekly appointments with Dr. Janet. Dr. Janet also had a weekly support group that she was going to try. She had her support network in place, one that wasn't dependent on Gwen. Laura figured she was as ready as she would ever be. Walter promised to be better about being home at night and on weekends. And she had promised she would work on her trust issues.

"I can't promise I won't ever be jealous of all of those nurses and doctors at the hospital, but I will focus more on me, getting myself healed," she told him. "I can't change the past, but I can try for a better tomorrow."

"I'll try too. No more escaping into work."

"I don't blame you. If I could have escaped me, I would have. Guess that was what I've been trying to do all along. How can I blame you for doing the same thing?"

At her last meeting with Pastor Joe, he urged her to spend more time with Jesus. She was beginning to look forward to this time and her weekly "word." Jesus didn't talk much. Usually he just gave her one word; sometimes it was the same word as the last week. But she could live on that word for weeks. She was still relishing her first word, "rest." She never imagined how wonderful it could feel to truly rest, found it hard to realize how little true rest she had known in her life before this time. Sometimes there was no word, and that was okay, too. She rested in his gaze.

She was working on ABC Please for DBT (Dialectical Behavioral Therapy)—Accumulate positive emotions; Build mastery; Cope ahead of time for emotional situations; and Please take care of your mind by taking care of your body.

Accumulate positive emotions – With Dr. Janet's help, she came up with a list of easy activities that she could do that she enjoyed and evoked positive feelings. Nothing too taxing to her body. Simple actions and activities that gave her pleasure in order to build up her supply of positive emotions. Things like putting up a bird feeder and sitting in the window watching the birds. Going for a walk on a sunny day. Calling friends.

"Don't call the negative people in your life," Dr. Janet told her. "They will only deplete your store of positive emotions. Stick with positive people, people who build you up rather than tear you down." Laura struggled at first to come up with these people. She had been out of circulation for so long, it was hard to come up with a friend list. So many of the friends she had made when they first moved here, back when Gwen was little, had slipped away. She decided to start with people she met at the support group who talked the same language and committed to reaching out to church members, couples she and Walter had been friends with in the past. She made a point of being up on Sunday and going to church with Walter even if it used her last reserve of energy. Church was a positive in her life so it became a priority.

Build mastery—Laura struggled with this. She didn't feel passionate about anything in her life. She had enjoyed her time working as secretary, but that had been so long ago. Maybe she could take some courses to improve her computer skills—a requirement in today's work environment. Maybe as she built mastery in one area, a passion would surface, she told herself. Fake it till you make it.

Cope ahead of time—Laura had once been the ultimate planner and organizer. Part of this was from her fear of being found out to be incompetent. She had organized her life, her husband's life, her children's life, trying to control all aspects till she had let go of all of this. It had felt good to give everything up, to sink into depression where no one expected anything of her. But now there was a price to pay in terms of broken relationships. She would try to heal those relationships one by one, starting with her husband and daughter. Then she would reach out to her estranged sons and daughter and her parents. But she would plan for these potential emotional land mines, make sure her store of positive emotions was full, before taking them on, lest she fall back into depression.

And, finally, please take care of your mind by taking care of your body. Why was this so hard? The last thing she wanted to do while in a dark mood was to eat healthy. No, give her chocolate and carbohydrates, chips and pizza. Not exactly a diet of champions. It was hard enough to push through her tiredness in order to exercise. And then to eat a healthy salad – impossible.

"You don't have to do this all at once," Dr. Janet kept reassuring her. "Remember, it's a process. We are looking for progress, not overnight change. As you eat better and take steps toward physical health, your emotional health will follow. Steps on a ladder. You just have to keep at it, one step at a time. And if you backslide, don't beat yourself up. That will only push you further down the ladder of recovery. Be kind to yourself. Be your own best friend. And build up that store of positive emotion."

Dr. Janet was beginning to sound like a Hallmark card, Laura thought. Still, she agreed to try.

"That's all I ask," Dr. Janet told her. "We start with accepting ourselves where we are, then take small steps to recovery."

Since being home, Laura hardly saw Gwen. Laura resisted any recriminatory words that would sound like guilt bombs.

"What time will you be home?" Laura asked Gwen over breakfast as Gwen was speeding out the door for her Bible study.

"Don't know. Late. I might go to the library after work and study until rehearsals."

"You have to eat something."

"I'll grab a bite."

"Okay," Laura said, hoping she didn't sound as disappointed as she felt. "I was thinking maybe we could talk some time. Maybe meet for lunch. Or maybe I could bring lunch to you at work?"

"Not right now, Mom. Not till the play is over ... and maybe not after that. Not till I graduate. I just won't have any time till then."

"Okay," Laura said. Time to rely on that store of positive emotions she told herself.

Chapter 35

Gwen rushed out the door. She hated this feeling of letting her mom down, hated the sound of disappointment in her mom's voice. Her mom was trying to hide it, but Gwen knew better. Her mom was trying to trap her in a web of guilt, pull her back to her where there would be no escape. Gwen would not give in, not now when she was so close to graduation and her ultimate goal of freedom was on the horizon. She just had to get through the last months of school, graduate and be on her way.

"I hear your mom is doing better," a church member stopped at Gwen's desk to chat after a church meeting. How did this woman know her mom was doing better? She had told no one. Her dad told no one. It wasn't something they talked about. "I saw her in the grocery store," she added.

"Oh," Gwen said. What had her mom said?

"You must be happy to have her back home."

Too much. Mom had said too much. She didn't want this woman's sympathy, didn't want anyone's sympathy.

"Yeah, well I've got a lot to do." Gwen tried to dismiss the woman. The woman persisted.

"It must have been hard while she was gone."

"What do you know? You don't know the half of it. You don't know anything about me or my life or my mother." Gwen's voice rose. She had to get rid of this woman.

"Oh, I'm sorry. I was just asking."

Pastor Joe appeared at the office door. "Is everything all right?"

"Nothing, Pastor. I'm just leaving." The woman slipped out the door.

"What was that about?"

"She kept asking me about my mom. It's none of her business, or yours." Her voice continued to rise. Gwen glanced at him then tried to hide her embarrassment.

"You want to talk about it?"

"No, I don't want to talk about it. Why does everybody have to 'talk' about stuff? I'm going to school, working, in a play and now I have to talk about my mom. No way."

Pastor Joe waited until she was done. "You want to talk about it?" he asked again.

Gwen was embarrassed when tears welled in her eyes. "No, I don't want to talk about it," she insisted.

"Come. Let's go to my office." Gwen followed Pastor Joe, still fighting back the tears. "Here," he pointed to a seat then sat down across from her. He pushed a box of tissues towards her.

"If I start crying, I won't stop," Gwen said.

"That's okay. I have the time."

"But I don't. I have work to do and homework to complete and ..." Gwen stopped talking in order to focus on fighting the tears. It was a losing battle. Gwen pulled out a tissue from the box and dabbed at her eyes.

"You know, sometimes it's more work to hold off tears than to let them flow," Joe commented. He waited while Gwen cried.

"You ready to talk about it?" he finally asked.

"What is there to tell? I'm over my head with work and now I have to deal with my mom."

"I know. I've been visiting her."

"What you don't know is my side of the story."

"I didn't know there were sides."

"Of course, there are. With my mom it's her side or no side. I didn't tell her to slit her wrists on Christmas Eve. I didn't have any say in that or in when she would come home. I'm tired of taking care of her." Gwen clenched the tissue into her fist.

"Is that what you are doing?"

"It's what I've been doing all my life. It's not fair."

"Unfortunately, life is rarely fair." Pastor Joe leaned forward and tried to meet her gaze. Gwen refused to raise her eyes.

"Well, it should be. It's unfair that I was born into my home with my mom. And it's unfair that some children are born into poverty like the children in Guatemala who live alongside a city dump. Neither of these is fair."

"Do you want to talk about Guatemala?"

"What's there to talk about? It's terrible."

"Some people would say you have it pretty good. At least in comparison to those children."

"Some people don't have to live with my mother. And I know, I'm so much better off than those children. I should feel grateful for all I have, but I just can't."

"Is this about your mom or the children of Guatemala?"

"Both, I guess. I don't know. Why is God like that?" Gwen raised her head.

"Like what?"

"So cruel. Doesn't God love us? Why does he let children suffer so? Why does he let my mom suffer so?"

"So, you understand that your mom has been suffering."

"Is there any way to avoid it? She wears suffering like her royal gown, demanding her subject's obedience."

"That's how it appears to you."

"That's how it is. You don't know. You don't know what it is like in my home. What it's like to live with someone who is depressed. And, you know, my biggest fear is that I will end up like her."

"Why do you say that?" Gwen paused and lowered her gaze before answering his question.

"Because lately, ever since coming back from Guatemala, it's been like there's a cloud over my head. I just don't enjoy life the way I used to. Sometimes I wonder if I ever did."

"Have you talked to anyone about this?"

"And be thrown into the psych ward with my mom? No way. I'm just going to power through this, graduate and get out of here." Gwen raised her eyes and met his.

"You think that will raise the black cloud?"

"It couldn't hurt, could it? Any place has to be better than here."

"And what will you do?"

"Go to New York. I've got connections there. I'll audition for shows."

"It's not that easy, getting parts on Broadway."

"I'll do off Broadway first. I'll wash dishes. I don't care as long as it is away from here." Gwen continued to squeeze the balled-up tissue.

"So, you'll run away to New York and run away from the drama that is your life rather than facing it."

"What else can I do? I can't stay here."

"Maybe you can stop acting and ask who you really are behind the mask you have created."

"And how do I do that?"

"By facing up to your past, making amends with your mother. Then go."

"Make amends? There's no amends to make. She's the one who should be making amends with me." Gwen leaned forward, placing her fists under her thighs. Everyone was on her mother's side, including the pastor.

"And that might be part of making amends. Allowing your mother the opportunity to apologize, if that is what she wants to, needs to do."

"I don't know, Pastor. It's always about her, what she wants and needs. What about me?"

"What about you?"

"I don't know what I want or need, but it's not this, not this conversation. I'm already overloaded and now you want me to do even more. Have you even been listening? How can I do more?"

"It can be awfully lonely hiding behind a mask."

"But safe."

"You can be safe and lonely, or take a chance, reach out, and maybe make a connection. It's your choice." Pastor Joe waited for a response. Gwen's response was to stand up.

"Can I go now? I don't want to deal with this, can't deal with this right now," she said as she walked out.

Gwen didn't like how she had ended it with Pastor Joe, didn't like feeling on the outs with him. It was a little like being on the outs with God. But then, she and God weren't on the best of terms either right now.

She had been planning on going to the library to study, but she couldn't study now. She pulled on her running shoes and started sprinting through the still partially snow-covered streets, the cold air burning her lungs. She ignored the tennis shoes dangling from the wire as she ran by. She refused to let them taunt her, remind her how she was still stuck here. She had to get away. Had to get out of this city. If not, she would end up like her mother.

Chapter 36

None was happier than Kathleen to have Esther and Peter return, and none more surprised as Kathleen at how happy she was. Esther and Peter came home directly from Florida instead of taking a more leisurely route along the gulf coast. Esther was anxious to get home and check on Erick. In order for Erick to come home, they needed to complete the ramp they had planned on adding in the spring. This just sped that process up. Dale had already purchased the necessary wood and other supplies. He had a work crew set up through the church to help him and Peter put it up. They were just waiting for Peter to get home and the snow to thaw.

"I'm so sorry you had to deal with your grandfather's fall by yourself," Esther told her over coffee.

"I wasn't by myself. Dale was around," Kathleen replied.

"You know what I mean. Your grandfather is going to be needing more care. Peter and I talked it over while we were in Florida. You shouldn't have to put your life on hold for him, or for us."

"What are you talking about, Mom?"

"I'm talking about—if you still want to leave Cascade Falls, you can. Wouldn't want you to stay here just for us. I appreciate that you stayed around for Josh and Scott. That's all I asked of you. You're still young. Time for you to do something for you. I know there's not a lot in Cascade Falls for you. I don't want you to stay because of me, or because of Joy's memory."

Kathleen was surprised when she felt tears seeping around the edges of her eyes. She couldn't answer her mother right away. She didn't know where the tears were coming from.

"What's wrong, Kathleen?"

"You've given up so much already. Raising Dale and me by yourself, then raising Josh and Scott, taking care of Grandpop. How can I ask you to give up even more, give up your dreams of travel? When do you get time for you?"

"Who says I want time for me? Taking care of others is what I do, what I love."

"And Peter is on board with that?"

"He wants me to be happy. I'm not saying we won't take any trips. I'm saying, you don't have to feel trapped here. Peter and I will take care of Grandpop and the Center. What we can't do, we'll hire someone else to do. You are free to leave if that is what you want to do ... What's wrong?" Esther asked when Kathleen didn't respond.

"It's just ... I don't know what I want to do with my life. I wish I knew."

"Have you tried praying about it?" Esther asked

"What?"

"Praying. Have you tried praying about it?"

Kathleen thought for a moment. "No, I guess not. That's for you and Joe, not me." She and God were on good terms now, but pray? She didn't do that on a regular basis, only during times of crisis.

"Sometimes it can help." When Kathleen didn't respond right away, Esther continued. "Ask God what God wants you to do. Maybe you'll get some answers."

"Okay," Kathleen finally answered. "I guess it won't hurt to try."

Kathleen didn't know how to start. This was Joe's area of expertise. She had relied on Joe when it came to anything God related, especially those times of crisis during Joy's dying and the years following. She didn't know where to begin. If only she could call Joe up and ask him. Instead she tried getting down on her knees beside her bed, the way she had as a child. It somehow felt right at first, but then as her knees began to hurt, she decided to shift to the overstuffed chair in her bedroom but this was too comfortable. It didn't seem right. She was afraid she'd fall asleep if she sat there for too long.

"So, sleep," the thought popped into her mind. "If you are tired, sleep, rest. I'll still be here when you wake up."

This was a novel idea. If she was tired, sleep. How did she know it wasn't the devil tempting her so she wouldn't pray?

"You don't." Who was this? How did she know who she was talking to? Was it just her talking to herself, fooling herself? Or worse, was it the voice of delusion and despair, leading her away from God?

"You know my name."

"Jesus?" The voice didn't respond but she knew she was right. Okay, time to try. "Jesus, what do you want from me?"

"What do *you* want?"

"I don't know. That's why I'm asking you." Why isn't he answering my question, Kathleen wondered.

"Search your heart." But how? Kathleen didn't know what she wanted, didn't know her heart's desire, didn't trust it. Doing what she had wanted had gotten her into trouble so many years ago. She no longer trusted what she wanted.

"Search your heart," the voice repeated. What was her heart's desire? For a moment Joe's face came to mind. Was he her heart's desire, she wondered, or was he in the way of finding her heart's desire? How could she know? She thought about New York, then Chicago, then Cascade Falls. No response. She thought about her family, her mother and brother, her grandfather, her sons, Joy. Tears filled her eyes.

"I don't want to feel so alone anymore," she said.

"And that is what I want for you."

"But how?" Kathleen asked. No answer. She knew what she wanted but she had no idea how to get it. Still it was a start. It was enough.

Chapter 37

The play, while not exactly a smash hit, was reasonably well accepted by the audience. They played to full, if not packed crowds. The applause echoed in her head. Gwen took her bows with the rest of the cast. She was pleasantly surprised to hear an upsurge in applause when she came on stage. They liked her? She had been considered too tall and lanky to be the leading lady and so had been relegated to the role of supporting actress. Her character provided comic relief. Gwen was surprised by the sound of laughter that accompanied her performance. It seemed she had a gift for physical humor, using her body for laughs. And a sense of timing and ability to deliver a line that awoke laughter from the audience.

It felt like her whole life, playing a supporting role to Marcie's leading role, playing the support cast in her mother's drama. She had been a side character providing comic relief to distract from the tension in her home. Seems she was good at it. But when would her own life begin? Certainly not as long as she was in Cascade Falls.

Her parents attended opening night. Marcie was coming for closing night. Marcie was going to the cast party then she and Gwen were going over to Marcie's for the night so they could sit up, watch movies, giggle and catch up on each other's life.

"It won't exactly be an exciting party, this being a Christian university and all. No alcohol. We don't have to stay late," she told Marcie.

Gwen was surprised to see her parents in the audience again for closing night. They came back stage with a bouquet of flowers.

"For our star," her dad said as he gave her the bouquet and hugged her.

"Dad, I'm not the leading lady, just comic relief," Gwen told him.

"You'll always be a star in my eyes. And some day the world will agree with me," he told her. "Besides, what would life be like without a little comic relief?"

"We'll see, Dad. Thank you for coming."

"Good to see you Dr. and Mrs. Thompson." Marcie joined the group.

"Marcie, let me have a look at you," Laura said. "Seems like only yesterday you were playing tea party with Gwen. Come over any time. How about tomorrow?"

"I don't think so, Mom," Gwen intervened. "Marcie has to drive back to school tomorrow."

"You can't come over for coffee and a bite to eat after church?" Laura insisted.

"Sorry, Mrs. Thompson. Like Gwen said," Marcie said.

"We're going to the cast party then I'm staying over at Marcie's," Gwen reminded her parents.

"Well, maybe another time," Laura said.

"Your mom seems better," Marcie commented as they walked away.

"Seems is the right word," Gwen said. "Come on. Time for some non-alcoholic punch."

Chapter 38

Kathleen was dreading this year's fundraiser dinner. Julia had taken it entirely out of her hands and turned it into something she didn't recognize. Gone was the simple catered meal in the multi-purpose room of the Center of the Arts at a price the parents of students could afford. Gone was the assortment of silent auction items, ranging from five dollars to fifty dollars. It was now a hundred-dollar-a-plate dinner in the ball room on the top floor of the hospital office building. Yes, Julia had been able to use her pull to get the place at a discounted rate, but it wouldn't be the same. And they were required to use the expensive caterers associated with the ball room as well as use their bar services. In the Center they had to purchase their own liquor license for the event, but then all of the proceeds for alcohol sales were profit for the Center. Kathleen wasn't convinced they would make that much more money. She heard from parents who had attended in the past but couldn't afford to attend this year.

"Maybe we can do another fundraiser in the fall, on a smaller scale," Julia suggested. "I don't want to leave anyone out, but the purpose is to raise money so we need to go where the big money is," she insisted.

Julia had already gotten a number of sponsors for the event, including friends and family from her hometown in South Carolina. The sponsors covered almost all of their expenses. Julia's dad considered himself a connoisseur of art and was donating an expensive piece from his own collection to the fundraiser. Her mother had donated a vase – pronounced with a short "a" – vase.

"Will local people from Cascade Falls know anything about those paintings, and if they do, will they have enough money to bid on it?" Kathleen questioned.

"We'll set a minimum bid. We don't want them to go for less than their value, but you'd be surprised what people will bid for something to support an incredible cause like this. Especially if you grease the wheels with some alcohol. That's why every ticket includes two free drinks."

"Maybe from where you're from, but this is a mostly blue-collar community."

"That may be. Perhaps I can get some friends to come," Julia suggested.

Great, Kathleen thought. Just what she didn't want. Not only was it entirely out of her hands, now it was becoming an event for some big money people from the south. Not what she envisioned at all.

At least Joy's picture was being put on display, not for sale. No price would convince her to sell the picture Sara had painted of Joy when she had been pregnant with Grace. Julia liked it too.

"The artist shows potential," she said as she gazed at the piece.

"And what makes you an expert?" Kathleen asked.

"My dad isn't the only art connoisseur in the family. He taught me a few things. Others I've learned on my own. Do you have any other pieces by this artist?"

"Yes, we do." Kathleen was pleased despite herself. She was pleased to know that she wasn't the only one to see the potential in Sara's artwork. Now if only Sara could see it as well. Sara had several pieces on display in the art gallery in the Center, along with other local artists. Kathleen encouraged her to keep painting, however with the twins and working part-time, she had little time for her art. Now that the twins would be old enough for pre-school soon, Kathleen was thinking Sara could get back into her art, but that had yet to happen.

"These are awesome. Does she have any more? Perhaps a piece we could use for the live auction?"

"You mean along with the pieces from your parents?" Sara's art was good enough to stand alongside this famous artist? She couldn't wait to tell Sara. It was hard to continue to dislike Julia after this.

"Yes. I think it will make an amazing opening item to start off the live auction, besides having the added appeal of being by a local artist." Julia continued to look at the art work on the wall. "Maybe we can get some other donations for the silent auction, but I want something from Sara for the live auction. What about entertainment?"

"We always have some of the dance students perform," Kathleen told her.

"That would be fine if this were a fundraiser for the dance studio, but this is for Joy's Center for the Arts. We need to show a broader appeal. Perhaps that incredible quartet from the music school, and maybe a scene from a play. Dr. Thompson's daughter is majoring in drama. She's part of a Christian Improv Group. Maybe they could perform. Something clean, not like some of those improv groups, but entertaining. I'll think about it."

"You don't want any dancers at all? What about the older students?"

"I'll think about it. Maybe a pas de deux. Do you have any gifted male dancers?"

"Not older boys. Most give up dance once they are old enough to start sports in school. My niece, Ashley, is a talented dancer."

"How old is she?"

"Twelve."

"I don't know. I'll think about it."

"You're going to have improv but no dancers? What is there to think about?"

"The entertainment is just a side. The main course will be the live auction. A side just complements the main course. You don't want too many sides. Dr. Thompson is an important member of the hospital community. We want to attract them."

"Well, my niece is an important member of the dance studio and Joy's daughter."

"I didn't say no. Just that I would think about it." So much for the goodwill Julia had gained from her interest in Sara's artwork.

When Kathleen told Ashley she wouldn't be dancing at the fundraiser, Ashley didn't mind.

"That's okay, Aunt Kathleen. I'd rather play guitar with my band."

"That's not an option either."

"Not this year, but when we are famous."

"Sure, Ashley." Ashley may not have been upset, but Kathleen wasn't happy.

The closer the date for the fundraiser got, the more Kathleen wished it was over. It looked to be a repeat of the hospital New Year's Eve ball. There was no way for her to get out of it.

"You'll help with the live auction, won't you?" Julia asked.

"Who's MC-ing the night?" Kathleen asked in return.

"I am."

"Oh, okay." Not that Kathleen minded not having that position. She didn't want to have to stand up and talk in front of all those snobs. Still, yet another piece taken away from her.

"You don't have to talk if you don't want to. Just help spot bidders."

"Okay." Not even good enough to say a few words at the live auction. Was Julia afraid she would spoil her big night?

When Kathleen said something to her mom about it, Esther encouraged her to talk to Julia about it.

"If you want a bigger part in the night, just talk to Julia."

"I do and I don't. I don't know that I want to stand up in front of all those people I don't know who don't know me. Or maybe they remember me, but the old me. I was so much more comfortable when it was just parents and friends of the dance studio, people I know."

"You want these people to become friends of the center, don't you? We need their on-going support."

"I guess."

"Just do it for the sake of Joy's Center. Do it for Joy. It's just one night out of the year," Esther told her.

Kathleen hated when her mom was right.

Chapter 39

Kathleen wore the same scarlet gown to the fundraiser that she had worn to the New Year's Eve gala. Julia offered her one of her gowns but Kathleen refused.

"I'm taller than you."

"Not by much. I'm sure we can find something that will look amazing," Julia said. "We can have the dress altered if we have to. I don't mind."

Kathleen refused to accept her charity.

"It's not charity," Julia said as if reading Kathleen's mind. "You are an important part of this night as the Executive Director. I want to make sure everything is perfect."

"Including me?" Kathleen said. "That won't happen."

"I didn't mean it that way."

"I know what you meant," Kathleen said and walked away. She may have lost control of every other aspect of the fundraiser but she wasn't giving up this one area of control. She just hoped no one remembered the gown.

She arrived early, pulling up her dress that was dragging on the floor in her flats. She had packed her heels for later, once the guests started to arrive.

"Okay. What do you want me to do?" she asked Julia.

"Nothing. It's all taken care of."

"Come on. There has to be something you need me to do. You can't be that organized."

"Okay. If you insist. You can check on the silent auction items. Make sure every item is clearly labeled and there are pens by the bid sheet. I'm going to check with the caterer."

Kathleen looked over at the bid sheets, all professionally printed, unlike the amateurish ones she had done in the past. She was disappointed when she didn't find a single error.

"At least let me help with taking tickets and signing people in," Kathleen told Julia.

"Taken care of." Everyone who arrived was being given a paddle with a number on it for the live auction and a bid sheet listing all of the auction items. "I want you to greet guests as they come in the door. Let them get to know you, mingle with them."

"Okay." Kathleen wasn't much of a mingler, at least not in this group. Go to a local brew pub or bar, she could mingle with the best of them, but here? She would have much preferred a seat at the registration table.

She switched out her flats for heels as guests arrived.

Julia had Chloe and some of the instructors taking care of registration and checking coats. Other board members were scattered throughout the room to help where needed, to answer questions about the Center and help guests find their assigned tables. Kathleen was disappointed when she realized she and Henry were sitting at the head table along with Julia and Joe. She had hoped to sit with her mom and Peter. Josh and Scott weren't coming home to help this year as they had in the past since they weren't needed. Kathleen was surprised when she saw Scott arrive, escorting a young woman with a milky brown complexion.

"Mom, this is Alex," he introduced his date. Julia came over and hugged Alex and Scott.

"So glad you were able to join us," Julia told them. "This is my incredible daughter," she told Kathleen.

"Your daughter?" Kathleen searched for the right words. She hoped her surprise didn't show on her face. "She's a gem."

"That she is." Julia turned to Scott and Alex. "You're sitting next to me, honey," she told them.

Julia formally welcomed everyone to the event. After her opening remarks, Joe said grace and the meal commenced. Kathleen looked longingly at the table where Esther and Peter sat laughing with Dale and Ava. She saw Sara and Larry join their table. When would she be able to escape? Julia's parents and Dr. Thompson and his wife, Laura, completed the head table. Kathleen struggled to make small talk with the doctor and his wife, who were across from them. She liked Laura. There was something genuine about this woman that she liked, down to earth.

Once Kathleen was able to slip away she went over to welcome Sara and Larry.

"So glad you could make it. You didn't have any problem getting a baby sitter, did you?"

Sara laughed. "It wasn't hard to convince mom and dad. We'll see if they are as eager after a night with the twins. They are a handful."

"Gabe goes one way and Angela goes another. You can't take your eyes off of them," Larry added.

"You'll be around tomorrow, won't you? I want to see those babies," Kathleen said.

"We're planning on staying till Sunday. Come over any time." Sara looked about the room and added. "This is a beautiful event."

"I know, a little pricey though."

"We got in for free because of the artwork I donated."

"That was nice of Julia. I didn't know she did that."

"We wouldn't have missed it, but we do have a tight budget with the twins and me only working part time."

"Did you see where we placed your pictures?"

"No, we just arrived in time to find our seats before dinner. Traffic was heavy out of Detroit and we had to drop the kids off so we were running late."

"Let me show you." Kathleen led Sara to where the live action items were on display. "You are going to be first."

"Wow," Sara looked at the piece donated by Julia's father. "This is a beautiful piece. Do you realize how much it is worth?"

"No, I don't know much about art." Kathleen looked at the starting bid. Twenty thousand dollars. "Who is going to pay that much for a picture?"

"It's a piece of art. At twenty thousand it would be a steal," Sara told her.

"You must be Sara." Kathleen heard Julia's voice behind them. Could she never be free of this woman?

"I am, and you are?" Sara said.

"Julia. We talked on the phone. I love your work. I showed it to my dad. He was quite impressed."

"Well, I'm impressed by this piece." Sara pointed at the picture she had been admiring. "How did you acquire it?"

"A friend of my family, or actually my dad. If you would like to meet the artist, that could be arranged. He likes finding new, young talent, as does my dad. I'll introduce you to my dad and he'll make the arrangements," Julia said.

"Sure, introduce her. After all, this is your big showcase event," Kathleen said.

"What are you talking about?" Julia asked.

"Nothing. Nothing at all. Not that anything I have to say matters," Kathleen walked away. She needed air. She took the elevator to the roof top and walked out on the gravel surface. The air smelled so much better up here, clean, cool. Better than the rarefied atmosphere inside. Below was the intermittent sound of traffic. Up here she could think, could breathe.

Kathleen walked over to the edge of the building and looked out at the city lights below. A few blocks away she could see the Center for the Arts building, shrouded in darkness. It was but a nub on the landscape compared to this building, but it was a beautiful nub. It was her nub. And now it felt like it was being taken away from her. It wasn't that she was leaving. They were being taken away. The Center, her friends, even her family. They were all being taken away from her by that blonde vixen. Sure, she wanted to leave Cascade Falls, but this was not how she wanted to leave. She wanted to leave of her own volition, not be pushed out by an upstart. Now that she felt it all slipping away from her, she was no longer so sure that she wanted to leave. Did she really want to leave her family? Leave the friends she had made through the dance studio? Friends she was making through the Center for the Arts? Now that the center was flourishing, there was no reason she couldn't go, but what if she wanted to stay? Would she have to fight for what was rightfully hers?

"Why don't you like me?" That voice again. It called across the rooftop. Would she never be rid of her? Kathleen turned around and confronted Julia.

"What are you talking about?" Kathleen responded.

"I have been nothing but kind to you since I met you, yet you continue to dislike me."

"Does it bother you that you can't win me over? That I refuse to go under your spell? I'm not so easily taken in by your deception."

"What deception?"

"You're all goodness and light. So helpful. So kind. People can't say enough about how wonderful you are."

"Everyone but you."

"Why does that matter to you?" Kathleen started to walk closer to her.

"Because," Julia took a deep breath before continuing. "You know the adage, keep your friends close and your enemies closer?"

"So, I'm the enemy. Is that because of Joe?"

"Potentially, potentially you are, but not because of Joe. You could end up being my daughter's mother-in-law. I don't want my daughter to be hurt. I want to know everything I can about you and your family."

"My son and your daughter? Come on. This is the first I even knew they were dating. I suspected he was dating someone, just didn't know who."

"This is not the first I heard it. That someone is my daughter. They've been dating since Thanksgiving weekend."

"That's not that long."

"It's long enough. I don't want my daughter making the same mistake I did."

"And what mistake would that be? My son is no mistake. You would be fortunate to have him in your family. Sure, he's no doctor or lawyer. He doesn't come from money, but he's a good kid, a solid, kind young man. He's a master plumber and when he gets his degree he'll be going into business with my brother. Reese's plumbing."

"Scott isn't the problem. I had to make sure he wasn't from white trash or worse."

"White trash!"

"Your background isn't exactly a stellar one."

"That's me, my mistake, not my son's. My sons, both of them, are so much better than I deserve. Just because I'm not perfect like you, doesn't mean my son doesn't deserve your daughter. I'm wondering whether you deserve my son."

"You take that back."

"Take what back?"

"Perfect. That I'm perfect. Take that back. I'm far from perfect."

"And what if I don't take it back? Perfect, perfect, perfect," Kathleen taunted Julia. Joe and Henry came out of the elevator as they fought.

"Should we stop them?" Henry asked when he heard them yelling.

"No, wait a minute. Let them get it out," Joe said

"Take it back," Julia screamed and lunged at Kathleen, grabbing her by the hair.

"I won't," Kathleen yelled back and reached over and ripped the strap holding up Julia's dress.

"How dare you." Julia ripped a sleeve of Kathleen's dress. Kathleen reached for Julia's perfectly coiffed hair and pulled it down while Julia grabbed Kathleen's hair.

"Okay. Now's the time to intervene," Joe told Henry. Joe pulled Julia away from Kathleen while Henry pulled Kathleen.

"What's this all about?" Joe asked.

"She called me perfect. I'm not perfect," Julia said.

"What's so bad about being perfect?" Henry asked.

"Everything. To be perfect is to not be human, to not be able to make any mistakes. I had to be 'perfect' growing up. I never lived up to the term," Julia said. Joe continued to hold onto Julia lest she lunge at Kathleen again. Henry restrained Kathleen.

"What do you know about not being perfect?" Kathleen said. "You with your perfect Southern home and your perfect family and your perfect hair and your perfect manners."

"What do you know about me? You don't know anything. I've had a far from perfect life. Did you know I spent weeks living in my car with my baby? Did you know that? You think I always had it easy. Did you know that Alex's father died before we could get married? He was in the military. He promised he would marry me when he came back, but he didn't come back. He didn't even know about his daughter. And my father, when he saw the baby was not 'perfect' – not white – he kicked us both out. Said I had to give up my baby or leave. So, I left. Alex's father's family would have nothing to do with us either. I stayed with friends, lived in my car, stayed at homeless shelters, lived on food stamps and assistance until I was finally able to get a job and find a place to live in that I could afford. And let me tell you it was not 'perfect' but it was all I could afford." Joe loosened his grip on Julia as she slowed down.

"I got a scholarship to school and was working my way through college as a single parent when my mom tracked me down and convinced my dad to take me back. Once he got to know Alex, he couldn't resist her. No one can resist those big brown eyes. She won him over. That was when she was three. Yes, my life has been better since then, but not always. My dad and I, we made up. He regrets the way he treated me and Alex. But don't you ever say my life is perfect. I've had heartaches you don't know anything about."

"Mom?" Alex spoke up from where she was standing with Scott by the elevator.

"Alex," Julia turned to face her daughter, "how much did you hear?"

"Enough, Mom, but we can't talk now. They are looking for you to start the live auction."

"Oh, no. I forgot. I'm a mess," Julia said.

"So am I," Kathleen said. "Let's go back by way of the stairs. That way we can sneak into the bathroom without anyone noticing. The rest of you, stall for us. Do whatever it takes." Joe and Henry looked at each other as their dates slipped off down the stairs.

"You heard what she said," Kathleen heard Joe say before she shut the door.

"We look terrible," Julia laughed as she held up the strap that had been torn, keeping it from exposing her chest.

"Speak for yourself. I never look better than when fresh from a good fight. Gets the blood boiling and puts some color in your cheeks." Kathleen was also holding up the torn sleeve of her dress. "What are we going to do about these dresses?"

"Safety pins. No good Southern debutant goes anywhere without them. You never know when you might have a ripped hem emergency, or in this case, a ripped strap." Julia searched through her purse for the safety pins. She pinned up Kathleen's dress, then pinned her own.

"Is there anything you can't do?" Kathleen commented.

"You haven't seen anything yet."

"What are we going to do about our hair?"

"No time to pin it up. I think it looks better down anyway, more natural." They combed out their hair and put on fresh make-up. Kathleen covered the scratch on her cheek.

"You got me there," Kathleen said as she applied make-up over the scratch. "I'm sorry I called you perfect, but you are so ..."

"Don't say it," Julia stopped her. "And I'm sorry I scratched you," Julia said as she continued to apply make-up.

"Not too bad. I've had worse." Kathleen pursed her lips and applied lipstick. "After this shindig is over, you want to have some real fun? I know a few good places."

"I bet you do. Sounds amazing. My daughter can entertain my parents." Julia put her make-up back in her purse and snapped it shut. "You ready?"

They locked arms and walked out together.

Chapter 40

Gwen had been waiting in the back with the rest of the students from her improv group while dinner was served. She glanced at the table where her parents were sitting and saw Marcie's dad was sitting with them, along with Kathleen, the director of the dance studio. She glanced about the room and waved to Ava who was sitting with her husband and a young couple she didn't recognize. She watched the drama playing out around her as she prepared psychologically for their fifteen minutes of glory. This might be a tough audience. Prior to this they had played to packed houses (because the space where they performed was so small) of students and parents and friends of parents. They had been favorably inclined towards them. They also included a lot of jokes only people on campus would understand. Their instructor had been coaching them all week to rid their repertoire of all such allusions.

"You have to know your audience," she had told them. So, Gwen was trying to know her audience and she was terrified. Not only was she facing her biggest critic – her mom – she was going in front of a whole room full of her dad's colleagues. What if she let him down? She gulped Vernors to settle her stomach. A beer would have done the trick more effectively. No drinking at a university-sponsored event, even though wine and cocktails were flowing freely about her. Under the watchful eye of Professor Gervaise, she couldn't get away with anything. It was the only drawback of going to a Free Methodist university, the no-drinking policy. She was glad her own church, the Lutheran church, had no such policy. Still, when in Rome ... She was following the rules, if not in spirit, at least in practice.

She watched as the director, Kathleen, left the head table and talked to the young couple sitting with Ava. Kathleen looked about as comfortable in this environment as Gwen was. Kathleen and the young woman got up and crossed the room. It looked like they were going to look at the auction items. Then the organizer of the event got up, Pastor Joe's date, leaving Pastor Joe and Marcie's dad alone. She wondered if she should go over and say hello.

It was obvious who the organizer was. She was everywhere. This was her natural environment. Her dad had told her about the woman, Dr. Julia Hennessey, now head of the oncology department. Was that her son sitting by her? Couldn't be her daughter. Gwen found her mind rattling as she prepared to get up and say hi to Pastor Joe and Marcie's dad. She was stopped by Professor Gervaise. "We're next," she whispered. "Get ready."

Dr. Hennessey came back with the young woman, seemed to be introducing her to the people at her table. Gwen didn't see Kathleen but didn't have any time to wonder about it as her group gathered for a short prayer the way they did before every performance.

The fifteen minutes sped by. The audience was appropriately receptive. There wasn't the cheers and loud laughter they were used to on campus, but the air was filled with chuckles and snickers. When Gwen looked around and saw smiles on faces, that was enough for her. They took their bows only to have Ava come up and ask them to do more. What was happening? The group of eight huddled for a moment as they picked out a routine.

"Let's do time warp," one member suggested. In time warp the audience picked three different time periods and two actors went through a time warp and met people from that time period. The pair of time travelers didn't know what time period they were entering and had to guess. Gwen was one of the time travelers.

"You up for it, Gwen?" her partner in time travel asked.

"Yup. Let's do it."

They did two more routines before finally being allowed to leave. Ava invited the guests to look at the silent auction items. "The live auction will be held shortly," she told them.

Gwen went over to her parent's table but did not see Pastor Joe or Marcie's dad.

"They went off somewhere," her mom said when Gwen asked.

"Tell them I said hi."

"You were delightful," said the woman who was part of the couple sitting with her parents. "We're Mr. and Mrs. Hennessey, Julia's parents, the woman who organized this affair," she introduced herself.

"Oh, pleased to meet you." Gwen was wishing she could shrink back to a more inconspicuous spot in the room. She wished she was short, like Marcie. Marcie could slip in and out of places without being noticed, but not her.

"It was so nice to hear clean improv. So much of what passes as comedy nowadays is nothing but filth and politics," Julia's dad said. "Not that there's much difference, between filth and politics, that is," he added, laughing at his own joke.

Gwen smiled politely. Her mother pulled her over to her. "If you'll excuse us, I have to talk to my daughter," she told the Hennesseys.

"Thanks, Mom," Gwen whispered.

"I met a lovely woman tonight, Kathleen Reese. Do you know her?"

"Some."

"You know she has two sons around your age. One is here tonight. Wouldn't you like to meet him?"

Gwen could feel her eyes rolling up into her sockets. Her mom had just lost any brownie points for rescuing her from the Hennesseys. "Mom, really."

"I'm just trying to make up for all those years I missed out. Isn't it my right to interfere in my daughter's love life and embarrass her?"

"What if she doesn't have a love life?"

"All the more reason to interfere. You aren't getting any younger. Do you know how hard it is for young people to meet any eligible partners their age once they graduate from college?"

"I know, Mom."

"Then how about the young men in your improv group. Why don't you introduce me to them? Certainly, there is one or two you are interested in. Invite them over to our home sometime." The teasing expression on her mom's face changed as Laura touched her daughter's hand. "I am better, Gwen. It's not like it was. You can have friends over now."

Gwen pulled her hand away. "Sure, Mom. I'll think about it." If only I could believe it, Gwen thought. Her mom did seem better this time, but she had been fooled before. She didn't want to go through that again. Just when she got her hopes up that her mom was better, she would come crashing down leaving Gwen with her heart broken once again. No, she wasn't ready to believe her yet.

"Gwen, the pizza's here," two members of the improv team came over to get Gwen. Their payment for performing was pizza and pop, provided in a separate room from the ball room.

"Gwen, who are these young men? Introduce us," her mother said.

"Todd and James, these are my parents," Gwen said. She raised her eyebrows as if to say, "Happy now, Mom?" Instead she said, "We've got to go," and made her escape before her mother could entrap them.

"Thanks for rescuing me," Gwen told them.

"Anything for a fellow thespian. You did look uncomfortable up there," Todd smiled.

Gwen saw Kathleen and Julia step up to the microphone as she was being whisked away. She wondered why their hair was down.

Gwen, Todd, and James were the last of the improv team left after finishing off the pizza. Professor Gervaise and the other members had left earlier. Gwen was feeling too wound up to leave just yet.

"You know, the only thing missing from this pizza is some beer to wash it down," James said.

"No kidding. Gwen, you're from around here. Where can we get some cheap beer?" Todd asked.

"There's a bar across the street. We can walk to it," Gwen suggested. "Though if you want cheap, then Jack's the place."

"Where's Jack's?" Todd asked.

"About a mile from here."

"Let's try across the street first. Do they have craft beers?" James asked.

"Always," Gwen told him. "Let's get out of here."

They were on their second pitcher when Pastor Joe and Marcie's dad came in with their dates. Gwen was so surprised to see them that they caught her staring.

"Crap," Gwen said as they waved in her direction.

"What's wrong?" Todd asked.

"My boss, who also happens to be my pastor, just walked in."

"You aren't at work and your church has no rules about drinking. Relax," James told her.

"Yeah, but they saw me. Now I have to go over and say hi." Gwen watched the foursome for a while. The two women were chatting away as if they were best friends, while Marcie's dad and Pastor Joe watched the clock.

"Hey, Mr. Taylor, Pastor," Gwen finally went over to their table.

"Hi, Gwen. It's good to see you," Henry responded. "Have you heard from Marcie recently?"

"Every day," Gwen said.

"More than I get," Henry replied.

"Do I know this lovely young lady?" Julia asked.

"We've talked. On the phone. I'm Dr. Thompson's daughter," Gwen said.

"Oh yes, the actress. I'm so sorry that I missed your performance. I was detained," she laughed and clinked her glass with Kathleen. "I heard you were amazing. Rave reviews."

"Thank you. I've got to get back to my friends."

"No, wait. Let me make it up to you. What are you drinking? I'll buy you a round."

"You don't have to."

"I want to."

"That's okay, Dr. Hennessey."

"Call me Julia. And this is my friend, Kathleen." They clinked glasses again.

"Thanks for stopping by. Tell Marcie I said hi next time you talk to her, and that I'm still alive," Henry told her before she returned to her table.

Gwen was preparing to leave when another pitcher of beer and a platter of chicken wings were delivered to their table.

"Courtesy of the woman over there," their waiter pointed at Julia. Julia raised her glass and smiled as they raised their beer glasses in response.

"We are crushing it tonight," Todd said as they clinked glasses. "What are you going to do when we graduate?" he asked Gwen.

"I have to graduate first."

"I need a road trip. We should all go to Chicago and try out for Second City," James suggested.

"Dude, that would be totally awesome," Todd said. "What do you think, Gwen? Should we give it a try? You're a natural."

"Would our humor fit? They aren't exactly a 'Christian' Improv group," Gwen said.

"We'll crush it. We can take what we have learned here and use it there," James said. "It will be an epic trip. There's plenty to do in Chicago."

"My friend Marcie is there. We could stay with her," Gwen said.

"Awesome. All we have to do is find out when they have auditions and go," Todd said. They spent the rest of the night talking about their upcoming trip to Chicago.

Gwen called Marcie when she got home, "I thought the woman your dad was dating ..."

"Kathleen," Marcie said.

"Yes, Kathleen … and the woman Pastor Joe is dating were arch enemies."

"They are."

"Then what about this?" Gwen texted Marcie a picture of the two of them clinking glasses and laughing at each other.

"OMG," Marcie said. "When did this happen?"

"I don't know. Maybe tonight. They didn't seem too friendly earlier."

"Got to be a story here."

"Marcie ... Remember last summer." Marcie had gotten into trouble last summer for writing local gossip on her blog.

"Just looking out for my dad," Marcie laughed.

"Oh, and some of my friends from my improv team and I are going on a road trip to Chicago to try out for Second City. Can we crash with you?"

"Like you had to ask. There's always room on the floor for your friends. When are you coming?"

"As soon as we have an audition date."

Chapter 41

Gwenn slept late the morning after the fundraiser. Her mother was waiting for her with coffee when she finally got up.

"Where's Dad?" Gwen asked as she accepted the cup of coffee.

"Called into work. You know your dad."

"Right. Well, I guess I better get studying." Gwen started to take her coffee to her room.

"You can't take a few minutes to talk to your mother?" Her mother indicated a chair at the table. "Sit down, drink your coffee. What do you want for breakfast?"

"Nothing. I ate plenty last night." Gwen felt like she was being set up. She started to plan her exit strategy.

"Nonsense. Breakfast is the most important meal of the day. Or, in this case, considering the time, you are looking at lunch. You can't skip both. What can I get you?"

"Okay. How about a bagel?"

"Cream cheese?"

"Of course."

Her mom slipped a bagel into the toaster, got out the cream cheese and set it on the table in front of Gwen, then sat down.

"Your dad and I were talking last night, on the way home."

"Oh," here it comes, Gwen thought.

"We are both so proud of you. We were thinking maybe as a graduation gift, we could go to Chicago for a weekend. Take in a show. Maybe go to Second City. Marcie could join us. Would you like that?" The toaster popped. Her mother got up to put the bagel on a plate, giving Gwen a moment to think. Was it a trap? Using Marcie as bait. Why didn't she trust anything where her mom was concerned? Her mom put the plate in front of Gwen, allowing her to spread the cream cheese herself, as thick as Gwen wanted. Gwen slabbed it on thick. She was hungry after all, needed to keep her strength up for studying. Finals were next week. She waited for her mom to say something about the amount of cream cheese.

"So? What do you think?" her mom asked.

"Okay. But first I have to graduate which means I have to study. I've got to pass my finals this week."

"Do you want me to see about making reservations and getting tickets?"

"Sure, Mom. Whatever you want to do."

"No, what do you want to do? This is about you."

"Do you really want to do this again, Mom? Since when has anything been about anyone but you?"

"Since I've been trying to do better, make amends." Gwen didn't respond, instead biting into her bagel. The cream cheese congealed in her mouth. "Will you ever accept that, believe that?" her mom continued.

"Look, Mom. I don't have time for this now. I have to study." Gwen picked up the cup of coffee and plate with the partially eaten bagel and prepared to leave. "And if the trip to Chicago is all about you wanting to trap me into a 'heart-to-heart', forget it."

Gwen hated how her mother kept trying to "talk" to her. She had had enough of her mom's talks when she was younger, only her mom's "talks" consisted of Gwen being the captive audience while her mom did all the talking, that is when she was feeling up to talking. She didn't care that her mom was trying to make amends. Gwen had heard that before. Why should this time be different from the other times? And why did her mom have to keep bringing this up now? If her mom had changed, she would recognize how busy she was right now with finals coming up and not bother her. No, she hadn't changed, Gwen thought as she climbed the stairs. What was important now was to study for finals and graduate. Everything else could wait. She sat her coffee and bagel on her desk, sat down and opened her computer. Still the tendrils of guilt tried to slip into her brain, taking it hostage so she couldn't study. The image of her mom sitting at the table taking deep breaths remained with her.

She had seen her mom pick up her phone before she left, wondered what her mom was doing, who she was calling. Gwen fought back, trying to wrest control away from the guilt, but it took effort to do so, effort she needed to study. Damn, Gwen stared at her text book, the words dancing before her eyes.

"Gwen," her mom called from downstairs, "I'm going out for a while."

"Okay, Mom," Gwen yelled downstairs. Good, Gwen thought, now she didn't have to barricade herself in her room to avoid her mom. She took her coffee and the empty plate downstairs, placed the plate in the dishwasher, then added coffee to the cold coffee in her cup and microwaved it. She looked out the window. The spring day beckoned. She longed to go for a run, or a bike ride with Marcie. But Marcie wasn't here. Instead she put her coffee in a travel mug, packed her computer and books in her backpack, left a note for her mom, and escaped to the library lest she risk being trapped by her mom again.

Chapter 42

Ever since the night of the fundraiser, Kathleen and Julia were best of friends. Kathleen visited her at the clinic on Wednesday nights and even helped out when she could. Julia visited Kathleen at the dance studio when she got out of work. They wanted to go everywhere together, including double dates. This was getting old, Joe thought. He didn't know what was worse: when they were fighting or now that they were friends.

"Can't we go out just the two of us?" he pleaded.

"I thought you were happy that we are friends."

"I am, but does that mean you have to spend all your free time with her? What about time for us?"

"I don't have a lot of free time and I don't spend it all with her. But that's okay. We don't have to double date all the time," Julia said.

The fundraiser had been the best yet for Joy's Center for the Arts. The initial count was well over seventy thousand dollars, thanks in a great part to the generosity of Julia's parents. The painting had sold for thirty thousand dollars, the vase for five thousand. Sara's picture had sold for five thousand, purchased by Julia's parents.

"Don't worry, young lady," Mr. Hennessey told Sara when she thanked him for the purchase. "I'm a business man. I see this as an investment. Soon this picture will be worth much more than I paid for it."

They had yet to get final figures. They had to get all of the expenses together, but there was definitely a reason to celebrate when Julia and Kathleen had insisted on "night caps" after the fundraiser. They had closed down the bar. Would have gone to another bar if they didn't all close at two o'clock.

"In New York, the party is just getting started at two," Julia said.

"And that's why I have to move there," Kathleen said.

"Move, why move? We'll go there together," Julia said. "I'll show you the town. Times Square, Central Park, Rockefeller Plaza. We'll take in a couple shows."

"Can we get soup at the Soup Nazi?" Kathleen asked.

"Of course. What trip would be complete without that?"

"When do we go?"

They pulled out their calendars and starting looking for a date, then gave up when they realized how few free weekends Julia had.

"I'm sorry I called you white trash," Julia said. Joe raised his eyebrows at this. No wonder they had been fighting. He was surprised Julia was still alive. No one could call Kathleen white trash and get away with it.

"That wasn't the words I was looking for. It was all that popped in my head at the time," Julia explained.

"What words were you looking for?" Kathleen asked.

"Well, something along the lines of drug dealer, criminal, shyster ... that's it! Shyster! That's the word I was looking for."

"I guess you wouldn't have been too far from the truth with those words. But white trash, that's a slur against my whole family. No one talks trash about my family."

"And they have no reason to. Scott is an amazing young man. My Alex is lucky to have found him."

"I wish I could say the same about Alex, but tonight was the first I met her. I don't know anything about her."

"We'll take care of that. I'll have you over for dinner this weekend."

"While your parents are home?"

"That is a problem. How about next weekend, when they are gone?"

"Perfect," Kathleen said. They both laughed at the word. Joe and Henry had to pull them apart in order to take them home in separate cars.

Julia hadn't slowed down as she had promised she would once the fundraiser was over. And then there was his secretary. He tried talking to her the week after the fundraiser only to be dismissed with the words, "Finals this week, Pastor. Can't this wait until next week?"

Joe agreed only to have her just as hard to reach the following week.

"Gwen, I'd like to talk to you."

"Sure, Pastor. I'll totally jump on it."

"Now. In my office." Joe knew that phrase. It meant, I'll saunter over to get coffee and stop and check my email and maybe respond to a tweet before doing what I said I would do, if I did it at all. Gwen looked like she was trying to come up with excuses, any excuse to avoid talking to him. He hated to say it, but he almost missed Marcie. Marcie had been all too happy to divert time from work to talk with him. Gwen was by far the better secretary, but with Marcie, she actually seemed to listen to him.

"What, Pastor?" Gwen asked.

"Now that finals are over and you're graduating this weekend, I was wondering what your plans were. Are you still planning on leaving Cascades Falls?"

"I told you when you hired me I would give you plenty of advance notice."

"I know what you said, but I also know, plans change. We can't always keep promises, even the most well intended ones. Life has a way of interfering."

"Are you trying to get rid of me, Pastor?"

"Not at all. I just wanted to know your plans. I also wanted to know how you are doing. You know that black cloud you were hiding from? Is it gone?"

"Why do you ask?"

"I'm not just your boss. I'm your pastor. As your pastor, I'm concerned about you beyond the job you do." It had been easier with Marcie. She had not been a church member. Her dad had been the member. This wearing of multiple hats was a challenge. His boss hat had him worried about having to find a new secretary when she left. His pastor hat had him worried about her welfare beyond the work she did. She was still a church member. He needed to help her find what was right for her, even if it meant losing his secretary. And then there was the counseling hat he wore when he met with Gwen's mother. He had to be careful to compartmentalize and keep the hats separate. He couldn't divulge anything from his meetings with Laura, couldn't let anything slip that might be considered a breach of confidentiality. Gwen knew about his meetings with her mother. Perhaps that was why she had become so reluctant to talk to him over the past five months. Or perhaps she was just burning out. Either way, he wanted to know. He hated juggling his many hats. Clearly this was why some in seminary recommended you not hire a church member for any position, especially secretary.

"It can get too complicated. And then, if there are problems with a beloved, long-term secretary and a new pastor ... Easier to have someone with no connection to the church," Joe remembered being told.

"Are you doing okay, Gwen?" Joe asked.

"Did my mother put you up to this?"

"No, I was wondering because when we met back in April, you talked about being depressed. Has that changed?"

"I wish people would stop asking me that. I'm not my mother."

"I didn't say you were. Are other people asking you?"

"You didn't say it, but you were thinking it. No, others don't ask because I have them fooled. I'm as good an actress off stage as I am on."

"Is that what you are doing? Playing a part?"

"I've said too much. I can't talk to you about this."

"If not me, then who?"

"I just know I can't talk to you. Can I go now?" Joe agreed.

Gwen didn't know who to talk to. She knew she couldn't talk to Pastor Joe because he talked to her mother. She didn't want her mother to know. It was her mom she needed to talk about. She couldn't talk to her mom, couldn't talk to her pastor, and Marcie was four hours away.

This was not something to discuss over the phone. She had told herself that once classes were done, once her senior project was submitted, once she was no longer involved with play rehearsals and performances, she would collapse for a while, get some rest. She needed a vacation, some me time. Then she would feel better she told herself; but instead, without all of the demands she had placed on herself, she was lost. She didn't just want to sleep for a few days, she wanted to sleep forever. If she didn't have work, she just may have done that — sleep away her days, sleep away her life. She had been waiting so long for this one goal, to graduate, and now it was over. She had reached it. What was she to do next?

She was lost. Her life felt empty. But who could she talk to? She remembered the staff advisor for the winter semester. Maybe she could talk to her? She had seemed nice. She had facilitated follow-up sessions for a while after the trip to see how everyone was doing, help them integrate the experience into their life. Gwen had not talked during these sessions but realized she wanted to talk now. She called Professor Peregrine and set up an appointment for later that week.

Gwen didn't know where to start when she came for the appointment. She looked about the office. Shelves of books lined the walls, many on spirituality and religion. Professor Peregrine didn't teach in the religion department, but it was understood that all of the staff at the college had a strong faith background. Professor Peregrine was in charge of cross-cultural studies. She had a degree in communications and one in spiritual formation. Gwen looked at all of the art work and pictures from the various sites where students did cross-cultural trips. Professor Peregrine got up from her desk and had Gwen sit across from her in one of two seats set aside for a more personal conversation.

"What brings you here?" Professor Peregrine asked.

"Professor Peregrine …" Gwen began.

"You can call me Pam. You're almost a graduate."

"Pam," Gwen wasn't sure how comfortable she was with the informality. Pam waited. "It's just that, ever since Guatemala, something hasn't been right. Maybe I'm going through a quarter life crisis."

"Can you say more about that? As far as I know, you've been doing fine. Your grades haven't dropped. There have been no reports of problems. I try to keep track of my students."

How could she tell her, Gwen wondered? What should she say? "I'm good at hiding things," she finally said.

"What are you hiding?"

"How terrible I feel. What a terrible person I am."

"Go on," Pam encouraged her.

"I just ... I feel so lost, so angry."

Chapter 43

They were finishing dinner when Kathleen's phone vibrated. Josh. Kathleen excused herself to take the call, slipping outside onto the sidewalk in front of the restaurant.

"Hi, Josh. What's up?"

"Mom, it's Stephanie. She's in trouble."

"Why isn't she calling her dad?"

"She called me. She made me promise not to tell her dad. She did say it was okay to call you."

"Okay, what's going on?"

"Stephanie's in jail."

"What! What happened?"

"Drugs, cocaine."

"Cocaine? What was Stephanie thinking?" Kathleen turned and lowered her voice as people walking by on the sidewalk started to stare at her.

"That's what I asked her. She said she wasn't thinking. They weren't her drugs, she said."

"Clearly. That girl never thinks. What do you want me to do?"

"We thought maybe you could help get her out. You do have experience with this." Why did she ever tell her sons about her past? Will she never live that down?

"I'll see what I can do. Has bail been set?"

"Not yet. Oh, and don't tell her dad."

"You made that promise, not me."

"Stephanie will be furious if she thinks I told her dad."

"She can be angry at me." Kathleen put her phone in her purse and went back to her table. How to do this? How much should she tell?

"What's wrong?" Leave it to Joe to read her face, Kathleen thought.

"It's Stephanie. We have to go." Kathleen continued to stand as she waited for Joe to get up.

"Wait. What about Stephanie? Is she hurt? Why didn't she call me?" Joe asked, remaining in his seat.

"Because she called Josh. I'll explain, but now we've got to go." Kathleen turned to Henry as Joe stood up. "You'll make sure Julia gets home, won't you?"

"Of course," Henry said. Julia motioned to Kathleen to call her.

"What is this about? What has Stephanie done now?" Joe asked as they walked out of the restaurant.

"Give me your keys. I'm driving," Kathleen ordered.

"Tell me what is going on first." Kathleen stood in front of the driver's side of Joe's car, holding her hands out.

"Stephanie's in jail. Cocaine. You going to let me drive now?"

"I'm going to kill that girl."

"Precisely what I thought. Just so you don't kill us both first before we get there. That's why I'm driving." Joe handed her his keys and climbed in the passenger side of the car.

"What do you know?"

"Not much. Just what Josh told me. She was arrested for possession of cocaine. She didn't want Josh to call you so he called me."

Joe fumed in silence before speaking. "What is wrong with that girl? Why does she always end up in trouble?"

"She does have a knack for bringing us together, not under the best of circumstances. Maybe this is another ruse." In the past Stephanie and Michelle, had schemed to fix their dad up with Kathleen. Now they had moved on with their lives, or so Kathleen thought.

"Not likely," Joe muttered.

"Just trying to lighten the conversation a bit. Clearly it didn't work. Stephanie has better things to occupy her time than your love life now that she is in college."

"Like drugs."

"That's not what I meant, but it's not exactly the end of the world if she is. She's young, experimenting with new experiences. She's basically a good kid." When Joe didn't respond, Kathleen kept talking. "She'll come around. Look at me. I came around. Besides we don't know the whole story yet."

"And it took you how many years ..."

"Okay, not a good comparison. Will you never get beyond my past?"

"What?"

"My past. Will you never get beyond it? That's why you wanted to keep our relationship secret."

"You were the one who wanted it secret."

"You never disagreed with me."

"The one time I did, we broke up."

"Either way. My past, that's why we broke up, isn't it?"

"This is not the time for this discussion." Joe put an end to that conversation.

They rode in silence, the sun glaring on the horizon, making it difficult to drive the stretch of I-94. Kathleen hated driving this stretch of highway at sundown.

"So, what's the plan?" she asked. "We need a plan. We can't just show up and wing it."

"Maybe you better talk to Stephanie. She doesn't want to talk to me."

"First we need to find out the details. We need to know the charges, how serious they are. Were others involved? Maybe Josh knows more by now. Then, based on that, we talk to Stephanie, get her side."

"Maybe you can tell her how mistakes in your youth can follow for the rest of your life," Joe suggested.

"You just aren't going to let it rest, are you?"

"You just said yourself that what you did is following you."

"I'll think about it." This time it was Kathleen's turn to shut down the conversation.

As they got closer to their destination, Kathleen called Josh. "We're almost there."

"Who's we?"

"Me and Stephanie's dad."

"I told you not to tell him. Stephanie's going to kill me."

"Not if her dad kills her first. Do you know anything more?"

"Just that her two roommates were arrested with her. Stephanie claims it was their cocaine."

"So, the cocaine was in her apartment, not on her person?" Kathleen asked.

"Yes, is that important?"

"Could be. What are the charges?"

"Just possession."

"What do you mean, just possession?"

"There was talk of charging her with dealing."

"Okay, we'll see you in a few minutes," Kathleen sighed as she hung up.

"What was that about?" Joe asked.

"She's being charged with possession. She said it wasn't her cocaine, but her roommates."

"And ... I know there's more."

"There was talk of charging her with dealing."

Joe closed his eyes and let out a long, slow breath. "I'm going to kill her," he muttered.

"But she wasn't charged, just possession. I think maybe you better let me handle this." Joe didn't respond.

They walked into the station and found Josh.

"Any more word?" Kathleen asked as they hugged.

"Yes, they are going to keep her until the morning. She has a hearing set for tomorrow morning. Bail will be set then. I'm sorry I brought you here for nothing."

"Can we see Stephanie?" Kathleen asked.

"I don't know."

"I'll see what I can do," Kathleen said. She talked to the desk clerk while Josh waited awkwardly with Joe.

"I'm sorry my daughter dragged you into this," Joe told Josh.

"Totally fine. She's like my little sister," Josh said.

"All right, they are going to give us fifteen minutes, but just two of us." Kathleen rejoined them.

"That's okay, Mom. You two go."

Kathleen and Joe were taken into an interrogation room to wait for Stephanie. She was in street clothes since she was being kept in the "drunk tank" overnight till her arraignment the next morning. She was clearly not happy to see them.

"Dad, what are you doing here? I told Josh not to call you. Where is he?"

"They only let two of us in to see you. He's waiting outside," Kathleen said. She set her hand momentarily on Joe's arm to try to keep him calm. "Tell us — what happened?"

"Nothing to tell. My roommates, they've been dealing cocaine. I just got caught up in the sweep," Stephanie said.

"You aren't using cocaine?" Joe asked.

"No, Dad. I knew you would think the worse. That's why I didn't want you to know."

"I just want the truth."

"I'm not using. How stupid do you think I am? Besides, even if I wanted to use, where would I get the money? Cocaine isn't exactly cheap." Too much information, Kathleen thought. She looked to see how Joe was dealing with what she said.

"That's all I want to know," Joe said.

"But you knew about your roommates?" Kathleen asked.

"I suspected something was going on, but I kept out of it. I just mind my own business."

"Didn't you realize you could be charged if drugs were found in your apartment even if they weren't yours?" Kathleen asked.

"I guess I just didn't think about it. I've been so busy with school and work. Are you at least going to get me out of here?"

"Can't do that, Steph," Joe said. "Not till there's a bail hearing tomorrow. I'm afraid you are here for the night."

Stephanie's face lost its bravado as what they said sunk in. It wasn't the first time she had spent a night in jail, but that had been in Cascades Falls. This drunk tank was full of questionable characters. Clearly she did not relish the idea of spending the night here. Kathleen saw Joe's demeanor shift at this glimpse of vulnerability in Stephanie.

"Okay. I guess I'll see you in morning," she said as the guards led her away.

"Do you think she's telling the truth?" Joe asked after she was gone.

"I don't know. She's a little hard to read." Kathleen squeezed his hand under the table.

"I'm sorry you had to come all this way for nothing," Josh said when they rejoined him. "You can crash at my place if you want. Stephanie's hearing is at nine."

Joe looked at Kathleen. It was still early, only a little after nine o'clock. "No, that's okay. We'll drive home and come back tomorrow. It's not that bad a drive."

This time Kathleen allowed Joe to drive his car. They rode in silence the first portion of the drive.

"I'll go with you tomorrow," Kathleen told him.

"No need to. I can handle it."

"But I want to. Besides, as you know, I have experience with such things. You may need my help. Might as well put my past to good use."

"I might. Thank you." Joe kept his eyes focused on the road ahead. "You know, what you were talking about before, about your past following you. About your past being why we broke up."

"Yes."

"Your past does follow you. It's part of what makes you who you are. I think it has strengthened you, given you wisdom others don't have. It's not your past but what you do with it, how it affects your present, that matters."

"I don't think my past caused you to break up with me," Kathleen explained. "I think it caused me to act in ways that made break-up inevitable. I didn't think I was good enough for you, because of my past. Don't think I deserve love. I'm still paying for my past mistakes."

"And what about now? How long do you have to keep paying?"

"As long as it takes, I guess."

"Are you still thinking about moving to New York?" Joe changed the subject.

"Thinking? Maybe, but not planning on it."

"So, you think Cascade Falls might be okay after all?"

"I'm thinking, maybe what matters is the people. I would have to find a whole new group of friends."

"That you would."

"Good friends are hard to come by. And then there's family. Where would I be without my family?"

"Well, I'm glad you're going to be sticking around."

"You are?"

"Sure, Cascades Falls would be so dull without you stirring up some trouble now and then."

"Oh, I'm sure someone else would come along to keep you on your toes. Just wait till Ashley's older. I suspect she'll provide plenty of entertainment. That's reason enough for me to stick around."

"No one else would be quite like you."

"And don't you forget it." They rode in silence for a while until Kathleen said, "I've been trying to pray."

"Really? How is that going?"

"Okay. I guess. You know it's not as easy as it sounds."

"How so?"

"Well, God doesn't always respond right away, does he? He takes his time. When I asked Jesus what he wanted from me, he asked me what I wanted."

"That sounds about right. What did you say?"

"I told him I didn't want to feel so alone anymore."

"And now you and Julia are friends."

"Yes, but that was in March. Julia and I didn't become friends till May. God took his time. And then, how do you know it's God you are talking to?"

"There are different ways. That's where church, or a community of believers, can be helpful. People who can help you discern God's voice."

"This isn't a ploy to get me into church, is it?"

"No, I'm just saying, life's hard. It can help to have other people who know you, know your struggle. I know there are people who manage to live good, moral lives without a faith community, but I don't know how they do it. I know I couldn't. Life is hard enough. Why make it harder by going it alone? I'm aware of the problems in any church communities. Churches are gatherings of people, human people, fallible humans. We make mistakes. There's gossip and hypocrisy and misunderstanding, but that's humanity. I need community. It helps me feel not so alone."

"You know, at one point, when I tried to pray, I thought I saw you. I had to put you aside in order to see the face of Jesus. It was like, you were in the way."

"That happens. People, ministers, parents, anyone can get in the way between you and your God. We, ministers, are human, too. As such we are fallible. We try to lead people to God, but sometimes we can get in the way. Not necessarily because of anything we've said or done, though that can be part of it. Sometimes it has more to do with how the minister is perceived. You did the right thing. Anybody gets in the way between you and your God, they need to be removed."

"I didn't really know what I was doing. It just happened." Kathleen paused, "If I wanted to go to church — I'm not saying I do — but if I wanted to, how would I begin?"

"Just begin. Show up. That's all you need to do. You have people you can go with. Your mother, your brother, Henry."

"I guess. That is if I want to."

"If you want to. Entirely up to you."

It seemed nine o'clock in the morning was the time that all the hearings started. Joe, Josh and Kathleen sat through a number of other cases until Stephanie's finally came up. She was being arraigned along with her roommates. They vouched for her, confirming what she had said about the cocaine being theirs. She got off with a warning.

"See, my roommates aren't all bad," Stephanie said after being released.

"You still need to get different roommates," Joe insisted. "You were lucky this time. You may not be so lucky the next."

"There won't be a next time," Stephanie told him. Joe just looked at Kathleen. She shrugged her shoulders and gave him a crooked smile.

"Come on, let's get breakfast," Joe said. "We can talk about it then."

Chapter 44

The evening was still early when Kathleen and Joe left. Henry didn't feel like going home yet.

"You want to go somewhere for dessert?" Henry asked Julia.

"Dessert would be awesome," Julia said.

Henry took her to a local coffee shop with a nice assortment of desserts. "They may even have music tonight," he said. They took their coffee and desserts and found a booth close enough to the music to be able to hear, but not so close that they couldn't talk. The musician was an acoustic guitar player. He sang a variety of folk tunes and popular songs from years back. Julia smiled and hummed along to the ones she knew.

"You like this music? I thought you were more a symphony girl."

"I do like the symphony, but I like all kinds of music, jazz, rock, blues, country. There's a lot you don't know about me."

"I bet I know more than you think."

Julia turned aside and looked down.

"I didn't mean it that way. I'm not referring to the incident on the rooftop," Henry recognized his blunder.

"No, I'm glad you know about that, know about my daughter. I have nothing to be ashamed of. And my daughter, she's awesome. She's the most important person in my life. Do you have children?"

"Yes, my daughter, Marcie."

"That's right. The indomitable Marcie, the journalist, gossip columnist ... what else can I say about her?"

"I guess I have talked about her."

"Yes, and her fame precedes her. I've heard quite a bit about her but tell me more."

"She's the most important person in my life. I just wish she wasn't so far away."

"Any other children?"

"No, just the one. When you have a daughter like Marcie, you don't need any more."

"What about her mother?"

"Died a long time ago. It's a long story."

"I'm not going anywhere."

"Maybe another time."

"Okay, leave me in suspense. Any other relationships since then?"

"None worth talking about."

"Is your life really that dull?"

"Just the life of a simple, small-town attorney."

They talked and listened to music. Then, before they knew it, hours had passed without their even once mentioning their respective dates.

"Guess it's time to go," Julia said as the coffee place cleared out and the staff prepared to close up.

"It's still early," Henry said. "But then this is a Thursday in Cascade Falls. Everything closes at ten. They roll up the sidewalk. Only bar patrons and hobos inhabit the streets after that."

"Sounds like a delightful place, my kind of place."

"We could get a night-cap, if you want."

"No, I do have to work tomorrow."

"Oh, yeah, that, work."

On the drive home Julia noticed she had missed a call from Kathleen. "I wonder what that was all about. The problem with Stephanie," she said as Henry drove.

"Thank you. It's been awesome," Julia said when he pulled up to her home.

"At least let me walk you to your door." Henry turned off the car and got out, joining her on the sidewalk. "I had a nice time too. Maybe we could do it again some time." Henry felt his body lean in for a kiss — then caught himself. What was he doing? And he couldn't even blame it on alcohol since they hadn't been drinking. "Or not," he pulled back and shook his head. "Sorry about that. Almost forgot myself. See you around," he shook her hand then headed down the sidewalk. He thought he saw Julia watching for a moment before going inside.

He sat in his car and watched as lights turned on and off as Julia made her way through the house. He sighed then turned on the car and drove home.

Esther was surprised to see Kathleen up and dressed on Sunday morning. Usually she spent the morning in her bathrobe sipping coffee.

"Why are you dressed?"

"Because I'm going to church."

"You are?"

"Don't make a big deal out of it. I'm going to ride with you and Peter and meet Henry there."

"Whatever you say."

Kathleen didn't want to sit up front with her family. Too obvious. She had made arrangements to sit in the back of the church with Henry. Joe caught her eye and nodded in her direction when he saw her. Kathleen raised her hand slightly in response then buried her head in her hymnal as the opening song began.

Chapter 45

Saturday. No reason to get up. Might as well sleep all day, but someone was poking her. Gwen rolled over in bed.

"Mom, what are you doing?"

"Okay. I know the routine. You are not staying in bed all day. You are going to talk to me."

"Leave me alone," Gwen rolled over, pulling the sheet over her head.

"I'm not leaving you alone. You are getting up and you are talking to me, whether you like it or not. I will sit here until you get up." Her mother opened the blinds to let in the sunshine then sat back down and poked Gwen again, repeatedly jabbing her in the ribs, trying to make her laugh.

"It won't work, Mom."

"Remember how I used to tease you awake when you were little? Back then I could just pick you up and carry you with me wherever I wanted to go. Now I can't pick you up, but I can still poke you."

Gwen remembered those days. That was back before her mom had sunk into depression. Her mom would get up full of energy, send her brothers and sister off to school, then pick her up and take Gwen with her shopping, shoe shopping, clothes shopping, food shopping, or she would visit her friends or family members. Her mom was from a big family in Philadelphia. Besides her parents, she had aunts and uncles, siblings that still lived there. Gwen remembered playing with her cousins. Gwen didn't remember that much about where they went, just that she was her mother's captive. That had been before moving to Cascades Falls, before she had met Marcie. Gwen barely remembered the house before her present home. This house was the only home she knew, unlike her siblings who spoke fondly of their home in Philadelphia, playing with cousins and staying overnight at their grandparents. Why had they moved from her mom's hometown?

That's right, Dad's career. It had always been Dad's career. She wondered, how would life have been different if they had never moved? Would her mom have been different? Guess she'd never know.

"Mom, I'm not a baby anymore."

"Then stop acting like one and talk to me." Her mother pulled the sheet off of her and tried to tickle her.

"You know I'm not ticklish, Mom."

"I won't stop trying until you get up. Come on. I'll make you a mocha – my special hot chocolate and coffee."

"Okay, Mom. I'll get up. Just leave me alone." Gwen sat up.

"You promise you won't crawl back into bed as soon as I leave?"

"Sure, Mom. Just go." Gwen pulled herself out of bed. She looked longingly at the sheets. She yearned to crawl back in and cover her head. How dare the sun shine, she thought as she looked out the window. It just wasn't right. The weather should match her mood, and if it refused to, then she would close the blinds and wait for it to change, she told herself, but she proceeded to get dressed to meet the day.

"About time," her mother said when Gwen finally rolled downstairs. "I was getting ready to come back and pour water on you."

Gwen grunted as she accepted the cup of mocha from her mom and sat down. The aroma filled her senses. The richness of chocolate mixed with the bitterness of coffee as she swirled it in her mouth. So good.

"French toast?" her mom asked.

"Sure, whatever." Gwen figured she was up, she might as well eat. But that didn't mean she was going to talk.

Her mother busied herself about the kitchen. She seemed almost ... happy? Was that possible? Since when was her mother happy? Seems Gwen remembered a time, a long time ago. She remembered it as if from afar, as if it were someone else's mother back when she was five or six, singing along with the radio as she made French toast. She didn't know whose mother that was from long ago, and definitely didn't know who this stranger was in her mother's kitchen.

"Okay, Mom. What's up?"

"What do you mean?"

"What have you done with my real mom and when is she coming back?"

Her mother placed a plate of French toast in front of Gwen. "That woman is never coming back, not if I can help it."

"But can you help it, Mom? If you couldn't help it for all of these years, how can you help it now? And if it was in your power to do something before this, why didn't you?"

Laura sat down. "I know it's a lot to take in, to try to understand. I don't understand it myself. If I did, maybe I could have, would have, been better before this. I just know it feels different this time. I'm different. Why did it take so long? I don't know. Dr. Kremer says I have highly resistant depressive disorder. I guess that means I'm stubborn to my very core, even in my DNA, if that makes sense."

"So, you couldn't get better until you were good and ready?"

"No, that's not what I mean. That implies I chose to remain depressed all these years. I wish I knew what brought it on. If I could pinpoint the cause, then I could prevent it. Was it from unresolved issues from my childhood? I had a good childhood. Not perfect. No one has a perfect childhood, but mine was good overall, especially as I look back on it now. Was it because of moving away from my home in Philly, my network of friends and family? Maybe, but maybe the move just unmasked what had always been lying under the surface, awaiting its chance to appear. I just know that once it had its grip on me, I was powerless over it. There were good days. You remember those, don't you? I hope all your memories of your childhood aren't negative."

"It's hard to get to those memories. I guess they are there somewhere, but so many other memories get in the way." Gwen wanted to tell her mother what she thought her mother wanted to hear, but she couldn't bring herself to lie outright. She tried to sneak around the edges of the truth to come up with a believable half-truth. Some days she had no good memories from her childhood. Pam said sometimes that happens. When you first start dealing with negative memories they overshadow all the good. Eventually those negatives will shrink in size to be proportionate. Then they will no longer hold as much power over you. And then she'll be able to remember the good. Gwen hoped that was true. Based on this hope, she gave her mom this nugget of truth.

"I'm sorry, Gwen. I'm truly sorry. I know I don't deserve forgiveness. I don't ask for forgiveness. I know I can't ever make it up to you. I just hope you'll give me another chance."

"Another chance for what? To destroy my life as I watch you self-destruct? To be let down again?"

"No, but maybe we can forge a new relationship. Maybe ... we can be friends? Is that possible?"

"I don't need more friends. I need, needed a mother."

"Would you give me a chance to be a mother?"

"Too late, Mom. Too late."

"Then let me be a friend."

"I don't know, Mom." If she let her mom in even just a little, what would happen? No, it hurt too much. She wanted to believe her mom, but then would come the inevitable letdown. If she let her mom in just a little, her mom would want more, would try to be more. Gwen would be disappointed, hurt again, or, she may get all she desired, a mother who was finally able to respond to her needs. Dare she hope?

"No, Mom, at least not now," Gwen finally responded.

"Then I guess Chicago is out of the question."

Gwen had been putting her mom off about the trip to Chicago. She didn't answer.

"How about you go on your own? Take the train, meet up with Marcie, see a couple of shows. We'll pay for everything."

"That would be totally amazing, Mom. I'd love to see Marcie." Marcie was staying in Chicago over the summer, interning at the Chicago Tribune.

"Okay. You look into making arrangements." Her mom got up and started cleaning the kitchen as Gwen finished off her French toast. Guilt began to grab ahold of her. Gwen tried to push the guilt aside. She didn't want to act out of guilt, but out of love, that was what she and Pam had talked about the past week. After the initial meeting, Gwen started seeing Pam every week. Certainly, there was some remnant of love for her mother behind the web of guilt. Maybe she could push away her tiredness for her mom's sake.

"It's not your responsibility to save your mom. Your mother isn't your responsibility," Pam said.

"You don't know my dad, do you? Mom has always been my responsibility."

"Then maybe she needs to grow up, take responsibility for her own life. What would that look like?"

"If I was no longer responsible?"

"Yes."

"I don't know. It feels like a huge burden being lifted from my shoulders. But what would I do then? How would I relate to my mom? I've always been the responsible one. I don't know how to relate to her outside of that."

"Then maybe you would be free to start a new relationship, a relationship of equals. How would that be?"

"I guess that would be okay."

"Only okay?"

"I'm afraid to hope for anything more."

"Then okay is enough. It's a start."

"But what if she tries to hurt herself again?"

"Were you responsible for that the other times?"

"I guess not."

"Then you won't be responsible if it happens. Your mother is the one responsible."

"I'm sometimes afraid to tell my mom the truth. My dad, he always told me not to say anything to mom that might upset her."

"What kind of relationship is that? One that's based only on lies and half-truths?"

"You don't know my dad."

"Well, your dad is wrong. You can't form an adult relationship with anyone based on half-truths."

"But I don't know that I want an adult relationship with my mom. I don't know that I want any relationship with my mom."

"That's your choice," Pam had told her. Gwen remembered their conversation as she watched her mom. Could they have an adult relationship? What would that look like? Did she want one? So many questions. Gwen pondered them before speaking.

"Mom? You want to go shopping?"

Laura stopped what she was doing to look at Gwen. "You mean it?" She paused as if unable to take it in, then answered. "I'd love to go shopping."

"Then let's go." The offer of reconciliation had been extended and accepted.

Chapter 46

Try outs for Second City was not an option, Gwen found out. She had searched the website for information about auditions. When she couldn't find any, she had emailed them. Auditions were held every fall but in order to audition you had to be a graduate of an improv and sketch comedy institution. Gwen figured her one class and being part of the improv team wasn't enough.

"You can take classes at Second City. Just think of all of the great experience you'll get. Then when you're done, you would have an in for a position. Maybe you could even get into the one in Hollywood." Marcie encouraged her. "And if not Hollywood, Chicago. We could have so much fun. Do you think your dad would pay for it?"

The weekend in Chicago had been totally epic. They had gone to different performances at Second City, shopped along the Magnificent Mile, hung out in Millennium Park, visited the Institute of Art, indulged in Chicago style pizza, enjoyed the night life and finished off the weekend with an afternoon Cubs game. All on her parents' dime. Gwen stayed with Marcie in the apartment she shared with two other journalism majors. Marcie told her about her internship and showed her around the Tribune. Marcie had become the purveyor of a wealth of information on all things Chicago related: the history, the corruption, the poverty, as well as the hidden gems only those who lived and worked in Chicago knew about.

Gwen enjoyed it so much that she decided to come back, this time with Todd and James. They were equally disappointed when they found out about auditions. "But that doesn't mean we can't still go on a road trip," Todd said. And so, they had made plans to meet in Chicago for a weekend.

And then there was the summer cross-cultural experience in Chicago. Even though Gwen was now officially a graduate, she was still able to take classes. Gwen and Pam had discussed the possibility of her attending and Pam pulled some strings in order to arrange for Gwen to accompany the group as an assistant. Gwen was struck by the poverty of inner-city Chicago. It was one thing to experience this in a developing country, another to see it in her own country. Chicago was a city of many extremes, from exciting theater opportunities with Broadway touring companies as well as local productions, to multiple museums and artwork, beautiful architecture, and a city of extreme poverty ready to explode into violence. Gwen was intrigued by all of the possibilities.

"What is it about Chicago and New York?" Joe asked over dinner with Julia, Henry and Kathleen, another double date. "Why are so many of our young people lured away to those cities?" Joe was aware of his secretary's recent excursions into the city. He was still waiting for her to announce she would be quitting and moving away to either Chicago or New York. So far it hadn't happened. It was like waiting for the other shoe to drop. He figured the minute he let down his guard and allowed himself to get used to the idea of having her around for a while, she would be gone and he would be back looking for someone else to hire and train. Isn't that how it always works?

"They do hold their attraction," Henry agreed. "Marcie will never come back to Cascade Falls, not after Chicago. But then, if not Chicago, she would have gone somewhere other than here. There isn't that much to keep the young people here."

"Come on, it's Chicago. Duh!" Kathleen said. "Who wouldn't want to live there? So much going on, so much excitement." Joe knew that Kathleen was all too familiar with the thrills of Chicago life from her younger years.

"I don't know about Chicago, but New York is incredible. My parents used to take us there every Christmas. We skated in Rockefeller Plaza and saw a Christmas show. My mom and I used to go there for awesome shopping weekends in the summer," Julia said. "There's just no comparison to Cascade Falls, not that Cascade Falls doesn't have its appeal." Julia and Kathleen exchanged glances, shaking their heads as if to confirm how dull their respective escorts were. Joe figured it was their own private joke about life in Cascade Falls.

"How did we end up with these two?" Kathleen laughed.

"Just lucky, I guess," Julia joined in the laughter. "We need to show you two how to have a good time — right, Kathleen?"

Joe and Henry just let them talk. They knew better than to get between the two of them. When double dating, Joe and Henry usually ended up spending the night talking to each other. That was okay with Joe. Better than trying to avoid Kathleen. Ever since their drive to Kalamazoo a few weeks ago, Joe felt increasingly awkward around Kathleen. He wasn't sure what it was. They were friends, sort of.

"And now Stephanie is talking about going to Chicago when she graduates," Joe said.

"Do you want me to talk to her?" Julia asked.

"Would it do any good?" Joe asked.

Julia looked over at Kathleen who responded for both of them, "Probably not. That girl is going to do what she is going to do. There's no stopping her."

"Then why try?" Joe, if not resigned to letting Stephanie find her own way, was aware how counter-productive any attempt on his part to dissuade her would be.

"I could try talking to her. She just might listen to me," Kathleen suggested.

"No, I've got to let her make her own mistakes," Joe said.

"All any parents can do," Henry agreed. "Here's to getting our kids through college and out on their own, still in one piece," Henry proposed a toast. "Do you think it ever gets easier?"

"It already is easier," Kathleen said. "With the kids gone, I don't know what trouble they are up to. Sometimes it's better not knowing."

"I'd welcome some of that trouble now and then. Gets awfully boring, living alone," Henry said.

"Is that a proposal? Or a proposition?" Kathleen teased.

"Just an observation. You can take it however you want," Henry teased back. Joe watched the exchange then looked away when Kathleen caught his gaze. What was he thinking? He should have known Kathleen wouldn't want to remain single, or at least not want to live alone the rest of her life, especially if she was staying in Cascade Falls. What did he care? Henry was a good man. He was happy for her.

"But what about you, Kathleen? I thought you were thinking about moving to New York?" Julia asked. Joe waited for her answer.

"And leave my best friend?" Kathleen teased.

"Who says I wouldn't go with you? Or at least visit every weekend. I love New York."

"And leave us here?" Henry asked.

"You can come along," Julia said. "I'm sure there's room for another amazing lawyer in New York."

"And have to pass the New York state bar? No, thank you."

"Then come and visit. What about you, Pastor?" Julia always called him pastor when she teased him. He had found it endearing, at first. Now, not so much.

"Isn't this enough about New York?" Joe didn't want to continue the conversation. "Who started this conversation, anyway?"

"That was you," Julia said.

"Then it's time for me to end it. Now all three of you are ready to move to New York? Isn't it bad enough our kids are leaving?" Joe said.

"Why should they have all the fun?" Julia asked.

"Joe's right. Let's talk about something else," Kathleen said. Joe was surprised that she actually supported his side for once. Whatever the reason, he was glad for the change of subject.

"What was that all about tonight?" Julia asked Joe on the drive home.

"What was what all about?"

"You know. All that talk about New York. If I didn't know better, I'd say you still have feelings for Kathleen."

"What are you talking about?"

"Ever since that night you and Kathleen spent together because of Stephanie, you've been different."

"How so?"

"Don't pretend you don't know. You know what I'm talking about."

Joe did know but he didn't want to talk about it. "You're the one who insists on us spending so much time with Kathleen. You knew it would be awkward because of our history, but you insisted anyway."

"Then maybe we shouldn't double date anymore."

"Maybe not. I'm not the one who wanted to double date in the first place."

"Okay, agreed. No more double dates," Julia said as he dropped her off. "I want you all to myself," she added as they kissed. Joe shook his head as he walked back to his car.

Chapter 47

It started casually enough. Henry had come to the hospital on business. He ran into Julia and they had gone to the cafeteria for coffee. What started casually had become a regular routine, having lunch or coffee every Tuesday in the hospital cafeteria. It was all innocent, Henry told himself. Just two friends meeting for coffee. There was no talk of dating. Both respected the other's partner. What was the harm in this?

It was all innocent, until it wasn't. Henry was finding himself thinking more and more about Julia, more than he thought about Kathleen. It wasn't fair to either Julia or Kathleen.

"I have to break it off," Henry told Andy, the investigator he hired to help with cases and his friend.

"Break what off? If there's nothing going on, what is there to break off? You don't know whether she likes you. As far as you know, this is one-sided."

"But what if it isn't? What if she feels something too?"

"So, ask her."

"What if she says no?"

"Then you would know."

"And what about Kathleen? Is it right to keep dating her when I have feelings for someone else?" Henry wondered out loud. "But then, if I knew how Julia felt, if I knew she wasn't interested, then maybe I would be able to forget about her and focus on Kathleen."

"Yeah, but if you say something and Julia shuts you down, won't that make things weird between you?"

"You're right. What if she says no and it becomes awkward. No – it's better to not say anything at all." Henry had decided, but then it slipped out.

"What is this?" he asked Julia the next Tuesday.

"What is what?"

"This. What we are doing. Is it just two friends meeting over coffee?"

"What else would it be?"

"Yeah. What else?"

"After all, you're dating my best friend."

"Yeah, right, and you're dating my pastor."

"What else could this be?" Both laughed then stared down into their coffee.

"Well, I better get back to work," Julia stood up and prepared to leave.

"Me too," Henry got up. "Coffee next week?"

"I don't know. Maybe we shouldn't be doing this."

"What do you mean? There's no reason for us not to get coffee. I shouldn't have said anything. Is it going to be awkward between us?"

"No, not at all," Julia said.

"Then coffee next week?"

"Sure," Julia walked away, leaving Henry to watch her departure.

When Julia cancelled their regular coffee date next week, Henry tracked her to her office.

"What's going on?" he found her at her desk in the oncology wing.

"Nothing. I'm just really busy. Lots of paperwork," Julia pointed to the mounds of paper on her desk.

"That never stopped you before. Besides, you have to have something to eat. Come get lunch with me."

"We both know this is wrong. I shouldn't have let it go this far."

"Last week, you yourself said it was nothing. Just two friends getting together over coffee."

"I lied. I mean, you're incredible, but we are both dating other people. What can we do?"

"We can break up with those other people. Give this a chance?"

"No, not possible."

"Am I interrupting something?" Joe appeared in the doorway. "I thought we could get lunch."

"No, not interrupting at all. Henry just stopped by to say hi. Lunch sounds awesome." Julia escorted Henry out of her office.

"You want to join us?" Joe asked Henry.

"Henry was just leaving, weren't you?" Julia said.

"Yes, I have to go. We on for dinner Thursday?" Henry asked.

"Sure, I don't know why not," Julia said. "Right, Joe?"

"Sure, see you Thursday," Joe agreed.

"See you there," Henry said as he left. He looked back and saw Julia walking down the hall, talking animatedly, her arm wrapped around Joe's.

Chapter 48

Gwen continued to meet with Pam throughout the summer. At first, she had talked about her mom and dad, but then she started talking more about God and what she would do with her life. She had thought she had known what she wanted to do. Get out of Cascade Falls. But now that that goal was in her grasp, she didn't know what she wanted. She didn't want to just rush off without a plan much as that had appealed to her in the past. But life wasn't as bad at home as it had been. It was even okay. Her mom continued to be okay, out of the dark hole that she had inhabited for so many years. Gwen didn't know what all her mom talked about with her group, but it seemed to be helping. Her mom had explained to her about ABC Please so that now they had a common language they shared. Gwen understood when her mom talked about storing up positive affirmations and accepting herself. She could use these herself.

It seemed that as life improved at home, she was less angry with God, but she still had issues.

"I still can't understand why God allows so much suffering in this world. Why evil runs rampant."

"You're not the first to ask such questions. People have struggled with these questions throughout history. I can't give you simple answers. You have to struggle with the questions yourself. Those are good questions, beautiful questions, ones that you can spend your whole life trying to answer. What I can tell you is that God loves you."

"I don't always feel that love."

"Did you always feel your mom's love?"

"No, especially when she was depressed."

"Does that mean she didn't love you?"

"No, I guess not. She did love me, does love me, in her own way."

"Just because you can't feel God's loving presence doesn't mean God is not there."

"If you say so."

"I don't want you to agree with me just on my say-so. I want you to know through your own experience."

"But how do I do that?"

"Life will provide the opportunities if you are open to them." Gwen wasn't sure how open she was to such experiences but she did know she liked the cross-cultural work she was being exposed to. She wanted to do something more with her life. She found herself talking more and more with Pam about what she would do now that she had graduated.

"Have you asked God for guidance?"

"Sort of. But God doesn't answer. I wish I knew what God wanted from me."

"Another good question. Keep trying. Some questions are so big, they can take a lifetime to answer. They are big enough for you to live in them. You move inside them and walk around in them until you find an answer that works for a while. Then you get up and find another answer. Some questions, the answers are always changing. What God wants of you now, may be different from God's will for you ten years from now. That's okay. You just keep asking the question, living the question," Pam told her.

Sometimes after meeting with Pam, Gwen would go to the university chapel and sit for a while in silence. She asked God, "What do you want?" and waited, not knowing what she expected.

When she didn't get a response, she decided to leave only to hear a voice in her right ear say, "Follow me."

"Follow you? What does that mean? That could mean anything." Gwen wanted a clearer message. When she didn't hear anything more, Gwen took the words with her, holding them close, trying to understand what they meant, trying to use them as a compass to lead her to the next steps of her life. If only she knew where she was going.

"So, Gwen, have you thought further about what you want to do now that you have your degree?" It was one of those occasions when her dad was home to share a meal with her mother and her. Those occasions had become more frequent.

"I don't know, Dad. There's not exactly a lot of job opportunities for a drama major." Gwen waited for her dad to say, "I told you so." He had not been a fan of her getting a degree in acting, but as long as she took care of her mom, he had let her do what she pleased. He had even come around since seeing her in some productions. Gwen was surprised when her dad didn't tell her how he had warned her about such an impractical career choice.

"What about Second City? I thought you were interested in auditioning for them. Or other productions in Chicago."

"Can't. They require a degree from an improv and sketch comedy institution."

"What would it take to get that?"

"I could enroll for classes there. They offer classes, but I'm not sure I want to do that."

"Then what do you want to do?" her dad asked again.

"I was thinking," Gwen paused. Did she dare tell him what she was thinking? Would he consider it another waste of his money? "I could go into ministry. I could stay home and get a degree in ministry."

"But I thought you wanted to get out of Cascades Falls?"

"I do, or, did. The Lutheran School of Theology at Chicago has an awesome program for ministers. I could get a degree from them."

"And what would you do with that?"

"Be a minister, Dad. Or maybe mission work. I don't know yet. But I don't have to do that. I don't have to leave. It's not so bad after all, staying here. I could stay if you need me to." Gwen tried to sound convincing.

"What do you have to do to get in to that ... School of Theology?"

"Actually, I've already been accepted. I applied a month ago. I visited the campus when I was in Chicago for that cross-cultural experience."

"When were you going to tell us?" her mom joined the conversation.

"Maybe never. I just wanted to see if I could get in, and I did. Seems they think a drama major with a social work minor is good preparation for ministry. Who'd have thought? There is a lot of drama involved in church services. I have some courses I would have to take, pre-requisites, but they accepted my application. I can begin in the fall, or not. I don't have to go. I can stay here if you need me."

"Gwen, your mother and I have been talking. It was wrong on my part to make you your mother's care-taker all these years. She's doing so much better, and even if she wasn't, you need to be free to do what you feel called to do, and if that's ministry ..."

"But I could stay here and go to school here, if you want me to." Even as she said it, Gwen felt a sinking in her stomach. She had been surprised at how excited she had sounded to herself as she told her parents about LSTC. But if she was needed here ...

"No, Gwen. I could hear the enthusiasm in your voice when you talked about Chicago," her dad said.

"And I could see Marcie more and maybe take some classes at Second City," Gwen added. Dare she hope?

"If that is what you want to do, then do it," her dad said.

"Really, Dad? It's expensive, but I can get some aid."

"That's okay. Consider it back pay for all those years you helped out at home."

"Really, Mom, Dad?" Gwen got up and hugged them both. She hadn't expected this, had been afraid to even consider the possibility. Now it was becoming a reality. "Thank you! I have to tell Marcie."

"You do that," her dad said, sending her off.

"I'll miss her when she's gone," Laura said after Gwen left. "But it is the right thing to do."

"We'll miss her," Walter said. "But we'll be okay." Gwen had stopped on the stairs. She didn't mean to be listening in. She looked over and saw her dad take her mom's hand.

"When do you leave?" her mom asked over breakfast the next morning.

"Classes start in September. I have to tell Pastor Joe first. I promised him I'd give him plenty of notice."

"What will he do for a new secretary?" Her mom wondered out loud.

Chapter 49

Joe and Julia cut back on double dating but they hadn't given up their weekly dinners out. Kathleen would have wanted to know why and Julia didn't think she would be able to lie convincingly so wanted to avoid the conversation entirely.

Julia was unusually quiet on the drive to the downtown restaurant.

"Is something wrong?" Joe asked.

"No, nothing. What makes you think that?"

"It's just you usually have more to say."

"Oh," Julia said no more than that.

"Does this have anything to do with what you and Henry were talking about earlier this week?"

"No, not at all. Why would it? Can't a girl be quiet sometimes?"

"It's just not like you."

"Then maybe you don't know me that well."

"Maybe I don't." Joe focused on the road. Finally, Julia spoke up.

"You know, maybe it's not a good idea, having dinner every week with Kathleen and Henry."

"That's your call. You know my thoughts on the subject."

"Okay," Julia said and didn't say anything more for the rest of the drive.

Julia talked more than usual at dinner and Henry talked even less than he usually did. Kathleen looked over at Joe, caught his eye then nodded in the direction of Henry and Julia as if asking, "What's up with them?" Joe shrugged his shoulders. Julia stopped talking and looked down at her plate. Henry was particularly attentive to his dinner, hardly looking up during the meal. Julia got up and excused herself.

"You want company?" Kathleen asked. It was their custom to go to the restroom together in order to talk and giggle about their dates.

"No, not this time," Julia said. Kathleen looked at Joe again, her face a question.

"Is something wrong, Henry?" Kathleen asked.

"Nothing at all," Henry said then got up as well. "If you'll excuse me," he said and walked toward the restrooms.

"What is going on with those two?" Kathleen asked Joe.

"I don't know. So how have you been?"

"Good. I'm good."

"It's been nice, seeing you at church. How is that going?" Joe asked.

"It isn't half-bad. Not like I thought it would be."

"And how did you think it would be?"

"I don't know. I guess I expected a little more fire and brimstone. It's okay, though the preacher ..."

"Tell me about it. I hear he's an old fuddy-duddy, dull as a doorknob."

"Worse," Kathleen said and laughed. Then she looked toward the restrooms. "It's been awhile. Should I go check on Julia? I hope nothing's wrong."

"Let's give her a few more minutes. I wonder what's keeping Henry?" Joe tapped on the table then said, "So, how are your kids?"

"Good and yours?"

"The same, at least as far as I know."

"Why look for problems."

"Exactly." Joe rapped on the table again and looked at his watch. Then he looked out the window where there was some commotion going on. There was a couple standing outside in front of the restaurant window having what appeared to be a heated argument.

"Look," Joe pointed to the window. "Isn't that Henry and Julia?"

"Looks like them. I wonder what's going on. Maybe we should get them."

"No, wait." They watched as the two started drawing more attention to themselves. The diners close to the window were watching the display. "Maybe we better."

Joe and Kathleen got up and started towards the exit when clapping broke out across the restaurant. They went to the window and there were Henry and Julia in a passionate embrace. Joe tapped on the window to get their attention. Henry and Julia stopped kissing and looked at the people in the restaurant smiling and giving them a thumbs-up. They smiled back until they saw Joe and Kathleen. Julia smiled sheepishly and gave a slight wave of her hand. Henry dug his fists into his pockets and looked down. Joe and Kathleen went back to their table and waited for them.

"Well, that was an interesting display," Joe said as Julia and Henry joined them.

"I can explain," Henry started. "Well, no, actually I can't."

"I think maybe we better be going," Julia interrupted him.

"I don't think what we saw needs any explanation," Kathleen said. "It was pretty obvious." They paid their bills and went home, Kathleen with Henry, Joe with Julia. "Call me?" Julia motioned with her hand to Kathleen.

Chapter 50

Kathleen wasn't surprised to see a text from Julia before she got home.

"We've got to talk!"

"Will call you when I get home."

"No. Where can we meet?"

Katherine looked at the text and ignored it. It could be taken care of when she got home. Now she had Henry to deal with. Neither said much at first. Finally, Henry broke the silence.

"Are you going to say something? Anything?"

"What is there to say?"

"Would it help if I said I'm sorry?"

"No, but say it anyway."

"I'm sorry. I don't know what happened. I didn't mean for it to happen."

"How long has this been going on?"

"It hasn't been going on. It just happened."

"Don't lie, counselor."

"Okay. We've been meeting for coffee at the hospital. It was nothing. I ran into her while there on business. We decided to get coffee. Then it happened again and again."

Kathleen looked over at Henry as he drove.

"And …?"

"And … Okay, it started that night after you and Joe left together. We went out for dessert afterwards. But nothing happened. Not even a kiss."

"Until tonight."

"Until tonight," Henry repeated. "Are you going to yell at me? Because I'd like to get it over with."

Kathleen waited, purposefully letting him squirm. "No," she finally said. "I'm not going to yell. The least you could have done was tell me before this, rather than embarrassing me in public."

"I said I'm sorry," Henry glanced over at her before returning his eyes to the road.

"I guess I could be, should be, angry, but I'm not. I guess it was inevitable."

"What are you talking about?"

"I mean, it was coming. I like you, but, I don't know. I didn't see us going anywhere."

"And when did you decide that?"

"I think it was on New Year's Eve when you were so oblivious to how uncomfortable I was," Kathleen started. "I guess I'm just not cut out for life with a small-town lawyer."

"You've been thinking about this since New Years and never said anything?"

"I was just thinking. No decision had been made."

"You were pulling away from me long before I became interested in Julia."

"Now don't go turning this into my fault. You were the one who publicly humiliated me."

"Here I was, feeling like a schmuck, and you were thinking about breaking up with me. What were you waiting for? Someone better to come along?" Kathleen could feel the anger she hadn't felt before this, starting to rise from within her stomach.

"You're the one who blew this. It's over. You have my blessing to go out with my best friend."

"You pushed me away. I don't need your blessing."

"Let it go, counselor. You're getting what you want."

Kathleen waited as Henry thought about what she had said. "I guess I am. Can we still be friends?" Henry pulled into her driveway and extended his hand.

"Sure, friends," Kathleen accepted his handshake then slipped out of his car. She waited until he pulled out of the driveway before looking at her phone.

"Meet me at the brew pub," she texted back. "You buy." Kathleen figured she might as well take advantage of the situation. She started a tab and was already on her second beer when Julia arrived.

"How did it go with Joe?" she asked.

"Oh, you know Joe. He didn't say much, tried to be all pastoral and all."

"You going to try to work things out?"

"No. I did just publicly humiliate the local pastor."

"Yeah, the gossip network is probably going viral with the news." Kathleen cringed for Joe as she imagined pictures of Julia and Henry kissing, posted on social media. Maybe Joe had been right all along about keeping their relationship secret last year. Better than this. Julia frowned and looked at her beer.

"Yeah, that. What about you and Henry?" Julia asked.

"What do you think?"

"I'm sorry. I didn't mean for this to happen."

"That's okay. Henry and I, we weren't going anywhere."

"Why not? Henry's an incredible guy. So kind, sweet. He reminds me of the small-town lawyers back in South Carolina. A real gentleman."

"Maybe he's right for you, but not for me."

"Then who is? The good pastor?"

"No, we've tried. Won't work." Kathleen finished off her beer.

"That so? I think maybe Joe might have been relieved."

"How so?"

"He just didn't seem that upset."

"He's upset. Trust me. That's just Joe. He doesn't let on what he is feeling."

"I don't know. I kind of think he might still have feelings for you." Julia tilted her head and raised her eyebrows in a question as she said this.

"You and Henry, you're great together. Me and Joe … I don't want to go there."

"We still friends?" Julia asked.

"Sure, just keep the beer coming."

As the evening wore on and more beers were consumed, Julia started to go on and on about Henry, how amazing he was.

"Wait, you're starting to give me second thoughts about letting him go so easily," Kathleen told her as she stood up. "I've got to go. I wish you and Henry the best."

"And I wish for you what Henry and I have found."

"I wish that too," Kathleen said as she left Julia to pay the bill.

Chapter 51

Gwen knocked on Pastor Joe's door. "Can we talk?"

Joe looked up from his work. This was never good.

"Sure, Gwen. Come in."

Gwen came in and sat on her hands like she had not quite a year ago when she had interviewed for the position. Had it already been almost a year? Didn't seem possible. Joe never expected her to last that long. Joe waited for Gwen to start.

"You know, I told you I would give you plenty of notice before I left."

"Yes, you told me that."

"Well, I've been accepted into the Lutheran School of Theology at Chicago. I start school in three weeks."

"LSTC? That's great. But I didn't think you were interested in ministry."

"Neither did I, until this summer. I want to give it a try."

"And what about your acting?"

"That can be a side career, or a hobby. Besides, acting can make a sermon more interesting. You ought to try it."

"Maybe. Maybe a little improv wouldn't hurt." Joe smiled. How would that play out in this congregation? "When do you leave?"

"About that." Gwen shifted awkwardly, bouncing on her hands. "Classes don't start for three weeks but I need time to get settled so I was wondering … Would next week work?"

"Next week? That doesn't give me any time to advertise the opening, much less find someone."

"That's the best part. I have someone for you. She's older so she won't be leaving to go to school or moving away. She has experience as a secretary and is a church member."

"So, who is the person?"

Gwen handed Joe an application. "My mom."

A week later, Gwen was packing her bags into her dad's car and preparing for her drive to Chicago. She was leaving her car at home and planning to get around on the "L" or use the CTA bus – Chicago Transit Authority. It was all part of the "Chicago experience," according to Marcie.

Her dad took the day off to drive her there.

"I could take the train, Dad," Gwen told him. But he insisted.

"Don't deprive me of my right to move my daughter into her new place. It's a rite of passage." Her mom was busy learning her new job, under the skillful instruction of Edna.

Gwen looked up for the pair of tennis shoes that had taunted her for the last year, wanting to say goodbye, only to realize they were gone.

"What happened to the tennis shoes that were hanging there?" she remarked to her dad, not expecting that he would know.

"Those? I think the laces finally wore through from the weather. I saw them in the road the other day."

"What happened to them?"

"Don't know. Why do you ask? Do you know who they belonged to? They were pretty beat up."

"Nothing, Dad. No reason."

"I kind of miss them. It was fun to wonder where they came from."

"Me too," Gwen said as they drove away.

Chapter 52

Since that first time, Kathleen was now attending church every Sunday, sitting in back with Henry at first, then moving up front to be with her family once she broke up with Henry. Kathleen hadn't talked to Joe since that night. She wondered how he was doing but didn't feel she should ask. She kept her distance at church, acknowledging him when she left, but not talking to him.

She hadn't been sure about church at first, but she was becoming more comfortable over time. She started staying for coffee, began to make connections, and even signed up to help with coffee hour.

"I hear you have a new secretary," Kathleen commented to Joe while wiping down the table where the coffee had been.

"I do. Maybe this one will last longer than a year."

"At least she's not a college student."

"That is a plus," Joe said.

"I'm sorry about the break-up, with Julia that is." The hall had emptied out leaving Kathleen with Joe.

"You are?" Joe responded. "And I'm sorry about Henry."

"Wasn't meant to be. It seems we two are better at bringing others together than having a relationship ourselves."

"What are you talking about?"

"Ava and Dale, and now Julia and Henry."

"Maybe you're right." Joe started to walk Kathleen to the door. "You know, since we both are free," he stopped and put his arm on her wrist. "Will you ...?"

Kathleen gulped. What was he about to ask? "Will I what?"

Joe paused as if looking for the right words. Kathleen continued to look at him, waiting for him to speak. "Will you go out with me? Maybe get coffee?"

"Out in public, before all the world?"

"If that's what you want."

Kathleen stopped to think about it. "You know, we still have issues to talk about, don't we?"

"That will give us so much more to talk about, besides our kids and the center."

"Won't we just break up again?"

"Maybe, but what if we don't give this – us – a chance?"

"So many questions."

"Questions I want to explore with you."

Kathleen looked away from him as she tried to make sense of all of those question marks floating around in her head. So many what-ifs. What if they try and fail? What if they break up again? She didn't want to go through that. It had been hard enough before. Wouldn't it hurt even more this time? What if they actually made it as a couple? Dare she go there? She was far from the perfect candidate for a minister's wife. She and God were on okay terms, still …? But here was Joe, standing before her, asking her out, him with his low, caring voice and kind touch. What would a cup of coffee hurt? How could she say no when looking into those deep brown eyes? She looked back at him.

"I'm not exactly minister wife material. Julia was that."

"I'm not asking for forever, just a cup of coffee."

Kathleen bit her lip before saying, "Yes, Joe, I will go out with you."

"Great," Joe fumbled with his hands, unsure where to put them. He hesitated before adding, "Then, I guess, we can kiss?"

"Sure," Kathleen said. They kissed, tentatively, then laughed as Joe wrapped his arms around her and gave her a long, slow kiss.

"Let's get that coffee," Joe said as their lips parted.

They walked out of the church hall holding hands and laughing.

Note to the Reader:

Did you enjoy reading this book? If so, please leave a review. Your comments would be appreciated and mean so much to me in terms of helping others notice my book. You, the reader, have the power to make or break a book in this day of emarketing and social media.

Thank you so much for reading *Beautiful Questions*. Stay tuned for the next book in the series!

Patricia M. Robertson

Other Novels by Patricia M. Robertson

Dreamweavers – Dream again, wherever you are in your life.

Buying Time – Visit the peace movement during the Cold War era of Ronald Regan, SDI (Strategic Defense Initiative) and MAD (Mutually Assured Destruction).

Land of Deep Waters - Honduras, land of deep waters, a country torn apart by civil unrest, violence and poverty: Is it possible to go back?

Magnificent Failure - Is it possible to start over? Failures in the eyes of the world and their own eyes, Diane and Jake found each other.

Dancing Through Life Series

Dancing on a High Wire – What do you do when life knocks you off balance? Join Sara, Joy and Esther as each seeks to find a "new normal" and regain their balance on this high wire we call life.

Still Dancing - Some phone calls we love, others we hate, like the ones Pastor Joe receives from his daughter's school. Or the one Dale received at work, letting him know his wife, Joy, had fallen and was in route to the hospital by ambulance. Could her cancer be back?

A Slow Waltz - The road to healing from loss is a slow one, sometimes going backward and sideways before going forward. Sometimes the biggest barrier to healing lies within us. Join Dale, Kathleen, Ava and others as they journey to forgiveness and healing.

An Irish Slip Step -The Irish slip jig is set in 9/8 signature time, unusual and a little off balance, like life! Kathleen didn't know about the slip jig, but she knew about slipping up. As did Chloe's, whose life was knocked off balance by an unplanned pregnancy. And then there was that fiery red-head, Mary Helen, who fell in love with an American soldier. Was it a slip-step or one of life's fortuitous missteps that brought them precisely where they were meant to be?

Delicious Secrets - Pastor Joe's church secretary retired a year ago. Since then he has struggled to find the right person to fill this position. Enter Marcie, a twenty-something college dropout, trying to find her way in the world. A church secretary was the last job she would have chosen, but she makes the best of it by entertaining herself with real and imagined secrets about church members, until she stumbles upon a secret she would rather not know. Once known, there was no turning back.

About the Author

Patricia M. Robertson is an author, speaker and spiritual director, who is committed to helping individuals find God in their every day experience. She also is author of a companion non-fiction book to *Still Dancing, Walking with Families through the Dying Process*, as well as *Walking with Families through Grief,* a companion to *A Slow Waltz*.

She has written other non-fiction books and writes a weekly blog and monthly newsletter. She has a Doctor of Ministry and over thirty-five years of experience in ministry to families. She currently is enjoying her own love story with her husband, Jack, grown children and grandchildren. For more information about her ministry, go to www.patriciamrobertson.com.

Lyrical Dance

Esther leaned back into the car seat and sighed, "It was a good day."

"Yes, it was," Peter looked over at Esther and touched her arm.

The unbelievable had happened. Kathleen had gotten married. Had it really happened or was it a dream that would disappear with the dawn. It was miracle, one that had been in the making for over forty years. Sometimes God took God's time, but then God comes through in ways she would never have imagined.

If only Dale, Kathleen's dad, could have been here to witness the event. Esther looked over at Peter, the outline of his face barely visible in the dark car. Only married for five years, yet it felt like a lifetime. It was hard to remember when he hadn't been a part of her life. But there had been years, many years, over fifty, before he had come into her life. There had been Dale, and a long stretch of raising her kids alone, and then raising her grandsons. Still she couldn't imagine a time without Peter. He had become such an integral, essential, part of her life. She knew the lines on his face, the angle of his shoulders as he entered a room and quickly took stock of the situation. He didn't slip in unannounced like some, sliding into the shadows or corners. No, he didn't need an announcement. He entered a room and took command, his presence going before him.

She knew the thickness of his neck and chest and the roundness of his belly, expanding from too many beers. And yet, here he was, by her side, driving her home at night to the house they shared. She felt safe and protected in his presence. She was happy by his side. She didn't mind the role of side-kick. Rather, she relished it, reveling in the thought that he was hers and she was his, to have and to hold. Just like Kathleen had someone in her life now too. Something she never thought would happen.

No, she didn't need to be center-stage. She was happier on the side-line. The invisible hands that made everything happen, that raises children, kisses booboos, warms hot chocolate on a cold winter night and tucks in with a kiss. She was the one, waiting in the wings, cheering on others in her life. That was what she did. She had no need for recognition or acclaim, except maybe from those closest to her, and then all she needed was to feel appreciated.

And now she had this man in her life. Someone to look after, to care for, for the rest of her life. A project …? No, Peter would not be anyone's project, though he did need taking care of. First there was his cholesterol … She wanted him to be around for a long time.

Dale had not been one to take care of himself.

"You worry too much," he had always told her. But he had given her plenty of reasons to worry back then, until one day, he didn't make it home. She winced as the headache she had been trying to keep at bay all day came back with full force.

Peter reached over and took her hand.

"Still have that headache?"

"I can't seem to shake it."

"When did you take something for it?"

"I guess too long ago. Who can remember with all the excitement. I'll take something when I get home."

Peter squeezed her hand before letting go and placing it on the steering wheel as he turned into their driveway.

"Home," he said. "Time to get you to bed." He turned off the car and looked over at her. Yes, he was a good one, Esther thought. Just like Dale. She was blessed to have two loves in her life.

"Whatever you say," she wanted to tell him, but the words wouldn't form in her mouth. Something was wrong. The last words she heard was Peter calling her name.

"Esther, Esther …"